✣

Our Lady's Troubadour

Also by J. K. Knauss

Seven Noble Knights (Encircle Publications, 2020)

"Footsteps" in *We All Fall Down: Stories of Plague and Resilience* (Alhambra Press, 2020)

Trout Riot: A Legend from Zamora, Spain, in Eight Scenes (Açedrex Publishing, 2020)

And look for the
companion volume to *Our Lady's Troubadour*,
a novella based on *Cantiga 5: Empress of Misfortune*

✠

Our Lady's Troubadour

and Other Miraculous Tales
from the *Cantigas de Santa Maria*
in Honor of Alfonso X, *el Sabio*

J. K. KNAUSS

Encircle Publications
Farmington, Maine, U.S.A.

Our Lady's Troubadour Copyright © 2021 J. K. Knauss

Paperback ISBN 13: 978-1-64599-292-9
Hardcover ISBN 13: 978-1-64599-293-6
E-book ISBN 13: 978-1-64599-294-3
Kindle ISBN 13: 978-1-64599-295-0

This book is a work of fiction. All names, characters, places and events are products of the author's imagination or are used fictitiously, and any resemblance to actual persons, living or dead, or to actual places or businesses, is entirely coincidental.

Cover design by Deirdre Wait
Cover image: *Cantiga* 100, panel 4. Manuscript T.I.1 of the Real Biblioteca del Monasterio de El Escorial, f. 145r. RB. Patrimonio Nacional.

Published by:

Encircle Publications
PO Box 187
Farmington, ME 04938

info@encirclepub.com
http://encirclepub.com

Contents

Illustrations

Introduction

A Wise King's Favorite Book

In a narrow room off of a patio in a historical building in Córdoba, Spain, some twenty American university students totter elbow-to-elbow on pork-chop-shaped desks. I sit in the middle of the mild chaos. The music appreciation professor, Pilar García Entrecanales, feeds a cassette tape into a large music system along the back wall and pushes PLAY.

Do we recognize the song?

Of course we do. It's "America" from *West Side Story*, the Puerto Ricans' ode to the contradictory place of dreams we're all familiar with.

This is Spanish Music class. What are we doing with an American musical?

Professor García claps the rhythm out: 1 2, 1-2-3; 1 2, 1-2-3. We're required to find the rhythm, too, and after a few tries, the class claps in unison. Then we take the tempo down. "Now

I'm going to show you how this is a Spanish rhythm," says the professor. "I'm going to show you where this beat comes from."

Bowed string instruments exit the speakers on tendrils that will lodge in my brain forever, though I have no way of knowing that at the moment. Even without the subtle drumbeat, it would be clear this song also follows the 1 2, 1-2-3 rhythm. A baritone whose name I may never know starts to sing in medieval Galician-Portuguese, which none of us have any hope of understanding, and changes my life forever:

Como poden per sas culpas | os omes seer contreitos
assi poden pela Virgen | depois seer sãos feitos

It was *Cantiga* 166, produced at the court of King Alfonso X of Castile and León (Spain) in the thirteenth century.

The king's voice reached across more than seven centuries to find me that day. I've spent almost every day since answering that call.

Alfonso X (1221–1284) has gone down in history as *el Sabio* (the Wise) because he loved learning. He attracted a team of Christian, Muslim, and Jewish scholars from worldwide intellectual culture to his court to record the latest scientific advances for future generations. The books that survive from his unique workshop include treatises on astronomy, astrology, the properties of stones, history, wisdom, law, and—because the wisest men need to rest their minds once in a while—pastimes such as board games and chess and humorous poetry. These texts have influenced great writers throughout history. The astronomy inspired and informed Copernicus, and the law works affected decisions through the twentieth century as far afield as the American Southwest.

Alfonso's extraordinary literary output was part of his political program to unify his loosely confederated kingdom under the values of good sense, fairness, and loyalty. He couldn't limit his studies to the things that most piqued his interest, but was obliged as monarch to set down all aspects of life and how it should be lived in writing. He carried this compulsion for compilation through to his magnum opus, the *Cantigas de Santa Maria*.

The practice of writing down the miracles of the Virgin Mary reached its zenith in the thirteenth century, with important documents from most cultures in Western Europe. What makes the *Cantigas de Santa Maria* collection different? In short, it's the biggest and the best.

The *Cantigas* survive in four deluxe royal manuscripts from Alfonso's workshop, with musical notation and thousands of illustrations. The manuscripts have in common a two-column layout in a clear and careful French Gothic hand on sheep vellum with illuminated capitals alternating in blue and red.

- **To**: The first manuscript, signature 10069 in the National Library in Madrid, is the simplest of all the codices, and contains the least amount of material. It likely represents the first phase of the *Cantigas* project, and includes 129 songs with gold leaf and musical notation. It has no illustrations, but its quality is inferior only in comparison with the other codices. It measures an impressive 315 by 217 mm, highlighting its value and importance.

- **E**: The manuscript with the largest number of *cantigas* is held in the library of the royal monastery of El Escorial with the signature I.b.2. It's also known as the codex of the musicians, because every tenth *cantiga* is headed by a column-width illustration showing one or two men or women playing a variety of musical instruments. Its 361 vellum folios measure an ambitious 404 by 274 mm and contain the prologues and 406 *cantigas* with gold leaf and musical settings.

- **Códice rico**: Because of its deluxe planning, layout, and execution, El Escorial manuscript T.I.1 is known as the *Códice rico*, the "rich codex." Measuring 486 by 332 mm, it's the largest of the manuscripts and contains the prologues and 195 *cantigas* that strongly correspond with the first half of E. It was originally intended to total 203, but several folios are missing. The gold leaf and musical settings are accompanied by 1270 vignettes forming narratives to illustrate each song, many of which are miniature masterpieces. I will describe them briefly below.

- **F**: The volume intended as a second *Códice rico* is housed in the Central National Library of Florence, Italy (signature Banco Rari 20). It probably once measured the same length and width as the first volume, but someone who didn't record his reasons for history trimmed it to 456 by 320 mm. F is incomplete, with 104 songs, many of which are fragmentary, of the presumed two hundred, in a completely different order than in E. The illustrations present various stages in the workshop's production process, with some pages only containing the panel frames (see Figure 11), some with complete vignettes (see Figures 1 and 9), and everything between. The staves were ruled, but remained empty, with no music (see Figure 10).

The stories in the *Cantigas de Santa Maria* deal with people's interior lives as well as the most unexpected details of their exterior lives, and include people from every social class, from Spain to Europe to North Africa and the Middle East. Some of these songs are masterpieces of lyricism, others are solid narratives, and still others take humor to new heights. Each of the thousands of illustrations offers delights to appreciate from any point of view. The *Cantigas* constitute the largest collection of written medieval music ever amassed, with more than four hundred songs, and contain every Western musical style of their time. No other collection was assembled over such an extended period. It's thought that the *Cantigas* project began around the time of Alfonso's ascension to the throne in 1252, and it was only abandoned upon his death in 1284.

Given that the miracles were gathered over decades, the collection shows a particular type of evolution. The first hundred *cantigas* focus on retelling stories from the larger Christian tradition. In the notes at the end of this book, you'll see that the stories in *Cantigas* 42 and 67 had been written down many times before. The final goal for the *Cantigas* project may have been five hundred songs. Numerology occupies pride of place in many Alfonsine texts, and St. Mary's number was five. Her number magnified one hundred times would've satisfied the most obsessive celestial mathematician. To meet the demand for so many stories, the poets must've searched in more recent history and closer to home, because as the numbers climb, more and more miracles take place in Spain during the poets' lifetimes. In the 300s in particular, many of the lyrics claim to have "heard" about the story. These *cantigas* were the first and sometimes only time these recent incidents were ever written down.

Not every song tells a story. In the style of a rosary, the *Cantigas* punctuate the miracle stories with songs in praise of the Virgin Mary at every tenth *cantiga*. Although these are some of the most beautiful poems, they lack plots, so none of them feature in this book.

Some of the illustrations from the E, F, and *Códice rico* manuscripts are decorative, while the majority depict the events of the songs in a format we might recognize today as a comic book, with six panels depicting actions and reactions in a contextualized setting, and captions to ensure the meaning of the images is never lost. All of the images transmit rich cultural information about customs, technology, and fashion. Some have served as the basis for modern musicologists to reconstruct medieval instruments, enabling them to re-create the sounds of Alfonso's court. I've looked at what miniatures survive for each of the *cantigas* in this book, and they've provided inspiration for some of the juiciest details in the stories.

Looking at a *Cantigas* manuscript even today is a multimedia experience that vividly suggests the exciting ways these songs would've been performed at court (Keller, "Drama"). By including all levels of society in words, pictures, and even adjusting the musical style to the plot, the *Cantigas* take on a folkloric aspect. Here, we learn some of the intimate details of a medieval farmer's existence at the same time as that farmer raises his gaze to divine intervention for help. The characters in these stories actively participate in a kind of magical thinking that allows miracles not only to take place, but to be expected.

As I argue in my academic work, the *Cantigas* portray society as Alfonso X wished it to be. Although this world is full of perils, people with faith in St. Mary come out ahead, and the faithless are punished. The plots inevitably end with the law and order that satisfies a medieval sense of peace and justice. There are no unhappy endings here, though sometimes it might take some interpretation to accept the type of happiness on offer. The secular world in this collection is structured rigidly with Alfonso on top as king. Thousands of other characters, even animals, represent his faithful subjects, whose hard work, family values, and religious piety are practical assets to Alfonso's ideal kingdom.

In order to encourage devotion to St. Mary, the collection portrays her, time and again, as being capable of anything, more than any other saint. Skeptics in this collection are few, and always proved erroneous. One *Cantigas* poet seems to be playing with this black-and-white worldview in the refrain of *Cantiga* 333: "Connosçudamente mostra | miragres Santa Maria" (It is well known that St. Mary works miracles). After 332 songs, the collection's theme must've been unambiguously obvious, and I read a touch of "All right, already, we get it!" here. In the stories I've chosen for this anthology, I've added some subtlety and complexity for the enjoyment of modern readers.

Alfonso's involvement in this project was deeply personal. He makes frequent appearances in the texts and illustrations. Joseph T. Snow has revealed a loose structure to the collection achieved by drawing the reader's attention periodically to the identity of the king, the "master architect-designer" of the project, an unequalled concept in the miracle genre (Snow, "Self-Conscious References" 54, 65). For example, in this book, I've chosen to adapt *Cantiga* 321, in which King Alfonso plays a helpful role in bringing about a miracle for one of his subjects. He also appears to have composed a few of the songs in the first person, and in *Cantiga* 209, he demands one of the manuscripts be brought to cure the illness he's suffering (Figure 1). Of course, it works, bringing him back from the brink of death when the royal doctors had given up hope.

While secular troubadours of the twelfth and thirteenth centuries selected unattainable noble women to worship from afar in their poetry, in the *Cantigas*, Alfonso explains that for him, there is no better lady than St. Mary:

> *And what I want is to praise*
> *the Virgin, Mother of our Lord,*
> *St. Mary, who is the best*
> *thing he made; and for this reason, I*
> *want from today forward to be her troubadour*
(Prologue B, l. 15–19; my translation of the Mettmann edition)

This theme is carried through numerous songs and depicted graphically dozens of times in panels in which the king occupies the space one might expect to be reserved for the Church as the intermediary between St. Mary and her devotees in his ideal Spain. In his testament, Alfonso instructed that the *Cantigas* manuscripts should be kept in the chapel where he was buried, and the songs should be sung on high feast days. This final wish for the *Cantigas* solidifies their role as the king's personal ex-voto, written thanks for the mercies St. Mary had upon Alfonso. They also served as a physical monument to the king's personal devotion to the Queen of Heaven (Montoya, "El Puerto"; Presilla, 137-149).

It's not uncommon for scholars to remark that the *Cantigas de Santa Maria* was Alfonso's favorite book.

November 23, 2021, marks eight hundred years since Alfonso X's birth. I can't let this historic moment pass without making

Figure 1. *Cantiga* 209. King Alfonso X requests the book of the *Cantigas de Santa Maria* to be placed on his ailing body and makes a miraculous recovery. Florence manuscript BR 20.

a heartfelt gesture. I hoped to participate in conferences with Alfonsine scholars complete with museum exhibits and concerts, but most such commemorations have been pushed aside by the COVID-19 pandemic. Under these conditions, events that bring groups of people together must be avoided. Luckily, creative writing doesn't require crowds. I can think of no better way to honor Alfonso's birth and legacy than to adapt stories from his favorite book so readers today can enjoy them.

In order to preserve the idea of the rosary structure of the original *Cantigas*, I've written ten miracle stories based on poems in this extraordinary songbook. I selected *cantigas* to adapt using much the same criteria as the original compilers: I wanted to showcase not only the most interesting stories, but also include people from every part of Spain (and a few outside it) and every social class, along with their customs, concerns, and animal companions. Here, you'll get to know a young German man happy to marry his sweetheart, a rich landowner who lives along the pilgrims' road to Santiago, a poor but resourceful French woman, a young mother married to the lord of a castle along Spain's southern border with the Kingdom of Granada, an experienced Navarrese musician, a novice in southern France, an important citizen of Zamora, a Castilian warrior who doesn't want to go home, a poor widow with an ailing daughter in Córdoba, and a French bride bewildered at her husband's treatment.

There are, of course, many other diverse characters and locations in the *Cantigas de Santa Maria*, and many issues that are sensitive for us today, including race, religion, and (in)tolerance, could be explored in further adaptations of the stories. Even after nearly eight hundred years, Alfonso's favorite book has much more to offer.

My Glorious Bride

Cantiga 42

Germany, thirteenth century

Elsslin took my hand. "I've found this ring my mother gave my father," she said. We stood in the doorway, so I felt the thrill of risk that a neighbor might see us and start gossiping. "I give it to you now, Waltram, because my father says we can be married next Monday."

The ring slipped onto my finger and fit perfectly. Elsslin looked at me with so much hope and devotion, I wanted to take her into my arms and kiss her until she begged me to stop. But in the shadows behind her, I saw a tall form moving. Her father, a widower, lurked back there witnessing everything we said and did.

"That's great news," I said.

We squeezed each other's hands, beaming. Her father stepped out of the shadows.

"Go on, you can do better than that. Show me I'm at least losing my daughter to a real man."

I laughed nervously and embraced her, closing my eyes so it was just the two of us. "I'll always take good care of you, my love," I whispered into her hair.

"And I you." Her sweet tones seemed like music to me.

Applause all around us pulled me out of our hopeful dream. It seemed the whole street was as thrilled as we were.

"All right, leave something for the ceremony," Elsslin's father said.

I reluctantly left her side and paraded down the street to whistles and pats on the back. When I took the next turn, I was left alone to make my way home, but I still stepped lightly, caressing the smoothness of the gold ring, which encased the finger that had a vein that ran directly to my heart.

At home, my father and mother embraced me and wished me and Elsslin well.

"We were hoping this would happen," said my father.

"We didn't think it would be so soon," added my mother, wringing her hands. "How will we ever ready the feast in time? And do you think we can get word to your uncle in Nuremberg so he can come? I can't believe you're leaving us so quickly!"

My father enveloped my mother's shoulders to contain her worry. "I've bought a house on Church Street. I've had workmen fixing it up as they're able. Why don't you go down there tomorrow and see if it's going to be ready for you and your beautiful bride on Monday?"

I hardly closed my eyes that night with the excitement. The next morning, I was dreamily touching the ring as I wandered the city and wasn't halfway to the new house when I heard someone calling my name.

"Waltram! Hey, Waltram!" Five of my friends waved to me as they approached.

Reinbolt gave me a quick hug. "We hear you're getting married. My God, what are you thinking?"

"I'm thinking I want to spend my life with Elsslin. She's beautiful, if you haven't noticed, and my family approves."

"Pfft," most of them scoffed. I was probably making too much sense for them.

"What a waste of a virile youth!" mourned Sigbald.

I refused to feel anything but satisfied with the turn my life was taking.

Reinbolt stepped in. "How about we go play stickball one last time while we're all still single?" Sigbald had the stick and the ball. They'd probably been headed to a game whether they'd seen me or not. My friends' riotous agreement with the idea pulled me along, and soon enough we were in the churchyard. It was an open space where many townspeople strolled at certain hours of the day, just the right size for tossing the ball and running to catch it.

I hadn't forgotten about Elsslin's ring, though. It was so smooth and fit so well, I didn't want it to be bent or scratched while I was sporting with my friends. I hadn't brought a purse or a sack of any kind, and couldn't think what to do with the ring. And that's when I saw her.

They were rebuilding the church apse, and must've moved the sculpture to keep it safe from the construction works. I'd seen the Spiritual Queen with her Child on her lap in its niche in the church many times before, and thought it pleasant enough, lit only with candles because it was situated halfway between the door and the rose window.

But in the niche under the eaves, the daylight cast its full brilliance on St. Mary's white veil and golden crown, put a sparkle in her eyes, and made her placid half-smile look nothing less than divine. Her blue nimbus with red bursts seemed to turn on an axis like the stars in the sky. Her red cape and blue tunic draped voluminously over the gold-painted chair. She held her Child on one side of her lap, and the other hand held the orb of the globe between thumb and forefinger. The other fingers curved into her palm, but her little finger was elegantly raised as if she were attending a banquet.

It was the perfect place to protect Elsslin's ring. I looked back at my friends taking their positions and dramatically knelt before the statue, calling their attention.

"From this day forth, the other lady I loved means nothing to me," I said for all to hear. I wanted them to know that even though I was getting married, I still had a sense of humor. "I swear before God that my eyes have never seen anything so beautiful. So, from now on, I will be one of your servants. I give you this beautiful ring as a pledge."

I slid the ring onto the image's little finger, and it looked comically large and out of place. My friends' laughter egged me on, so I put my hands together in mock prayer and said, "Ave Maria."

I'd had enough of kneeling, so I stood, brushing some dirt and grass off my tunic, but my friends shouted something and came running to me and the image.

"What?" I asked.

Reinbolt took my face in his hands and turned me back to St. Mary's little finger. It no longer stood out. It curved into the palm like the others, locking the ring in place.

"St. Mary, save me!" I yelled, joining my friends' frenzy.

I reached for the finger to see if I could pry it open and get Elsslin's ring back, but it was fused into the hand with thick layers of paint, as if it had never been open. The statue's half-smile now seemed slyly haughty.

I looked to my friends for help, but they were gone. They'd run away and abandoned me. Instead, there was an elderly couple with arms linked, watching my manipulations with furrowed brows.

"Help! What do I do?" I asked them. "I need to get my ring back!"

"You gave that ring to the Queen of Heaven? It looks like she's accepted, son," said the man.

The woman took my hand and patted it. Hers was full of rings, unlike mine. "You belong to St. Mary now. You must join the Cistercians in the monastery."

"Immediately," added her husband.

"Become a monk?" I blubbered. Such a thing had never crossed my mind. "But I'm getting married on Monday."

"Say your goodbyes if you must, but there's clearly no other way." The woman let me go, and I ran from the churchyard, straight to Elsslin's house.

She opened the door, and her face lit up. "Waltram!"

I embraced her tightly and sobbed into her shoulder. "I'm so sorry, my love. I have to become a monk."

She pulled away. "What are you saying? You're not making any sense."

"It was this old couple in the churchyard. They told me I have to join the Cistercian order."

"That's nonsense. Have you lost your wits? You're going to marry me on Monday." She held my hand between hers and gazed into my eyes, making me breathe more deliberately. "We promised."

"Yes, we did," I said. I inhaled and exhaled, and already the terrible memory faded a little.

"Where's your ring?" asked Elsslin.

I stared at my naked finger, now unsure of what had happened. "I left it at home to keep it safe. I know how important it is."

"All right. Just remember to bring both rings to the ceremony."

"Are you sure? Maybe I should go to the monastery."

"Nonsense. Never think of that again. Do you want to know about the preparations we're making for the wedding feast?"

I sighed, letting out the rest of my confusion. "Yes. I'm sorry. I was on my way to check on the house my father bought us. Could you come with me?"

Her father said it was all right, and as we walked the rest of the way arm in arm, she told me about making arrangements with cooks and bakers and embroidering her dress with her friends and their mothers. I had never felt so relieved to have a decision made for me.

On Monday, we heard mass in the very chapel where the statue of the Spiritual Queen usually sat. No one in the wedding party had to go through the churchyard where the image awaited the renovation, and I was afraid to check whether the ring was still on her finger or not.

While Elsslin and her family made the other arrangements, I'd scoured the city for a ring like the one I'd lost. In the end, my father let me have one of his gold coins, and I took it to the goldsmith with specific instructions. Those hours of trying it on and handing it back to the smith until it finally fit like Elsslin's had were some of the longest of my life.

After the prayers, I went to wait outside the church door, telling myself I was nervous because I was excited about seeing my bride, and the feast, and the wedding night. I shifted both rings from hand to hand as if the smith had just finished hammering them and they were still searing. All my relatives—my mother, father, aunts, the uncle from Nuremberg, grandparents, cousins—came to stand with me. Through the crowd, my stickball friends waved at me.

"Hey, Waltram, I thought you were already married to a statue," Sigbald shouted. I held my breath a moment, but it seemed no one else heard. I was safe.

Elsslin entered the plaza with all her relatives chanting around her. She wore a blue gown and red cloak, both edged and embroidered with gold. She had I'm not sure how many layers of gold strands around her neck and a golden headdress that looked like a crown. The sun glinted wildly off the adornments, but Elsslin didn't need any of it to shine.

I focused on her smile and her sparkling eyes, said what I was told to say, placed rings on fingers, and had grains of wheat showered over me to great applause, and soon enough we processed through the streets. Just outside town, banquet tables were set up with bright blue tablecloths, trenchers, goblets, tureens, and what looked like hundreds of pitchers full of beer, with wineskins conspicuously stacked near the tables.

Since Elsslin and her family had put everything together so well, I gave myself over to enjoying the good wishes of both our families, music by jongleurs and something like music from our friends, dancing, abundant food, and plenty of drink.

Night had fallen long before Elsslin and I stumbled back to our house and accepted last gifts and hugs from our parents. When we were finally alone, we stripped down and climbed into bed. It should've been the first time I saw Elsslin like that, but the light was too low.

She hovered over my face. "Would you like to get some rest..." I was asleep before she finished the question.

But there was no rest to be had. My limbs felt overworked,

even in the dream. It was as if I were running, running away from something that never tired or flagged. And suddenly St. Mary stood before me.

I knew it was her because she was dressed exactly like the statue in the churchyard, red and blue, with a golden crown, and a blue and red nimbus that dizzied me with its spinning around her head. Her eyes were like burning embers, and she wasn't smiling at all as she unleashed her vigorous voice on me.

"Oh, my faithless liar! Why did you forsake me and take a wife? You forgot the ring you gave me."

She held up her hand, and the ring shone on her little finger. It fit as if permanently fused, forming a part of her radiance.

"You must leave your wife and go with me wherever I say. If you don't, you'll suffer mental anguish for all the days of your life."

I yelled and woke. I was drenched in sweat, and my neck was as sore as if I had carried on my back all the beer and wine I'd drunk. I hardly knew what mental anguish was, and now I was meant to suffer it every day until I died?

It was still night, but moonlight streamed into the window we'd left open, and I gazed on Elsslin asleep beside me. I must not have truly cried out, for she lay peacefully. I brushed her hair away from her eyes and felt her warmth. I couldn't leave her. She was my wife. No irate statue in a dream could tell me to stop loving her.

I left my hand on her shoulder and drifted.

The Glorious Virgin lay between us, atop the sheets. I could no longer see my earthly bride. St. Mary's eyes shed more cold light than the Moon, and she held the hand that had been resting on Elsslin.

"You're wicked, false, and unfaithful! Do you hear me? Why did you leave me so shamelessly?"

Her voice resounded with all the power of the heavens. It left no room for me to think, much less to answer. She twisted my hand painfully.

My mind's eye witnessed my life with Elsslin, and it was full of toil, hunger, and pain. Red and black demon figures plagued my every movement, and when it came time for Elsslin to give birth, her life flowed away on a tide of blood. The demons carried off her soul and the soul of our child. When I reached out to stop them, they burned my hands, and I could do nothing but weep.

I screamed soundlessly, and the scene unfolded the drama in a different way. I lived not with Elsslin, but in the nearby Cistercian community. The monks helped each other and saw that no one ever went hungry or cold, and they could even keep some pain away with the herbs they cultivated in their garden. There was no sign of any demon, only sunshine and fellowship. St. Mary herself accompanied us during the masses we sang in her honor. I looked down at my hands, and they were strong from a life of work. They had no scar from being burned by demons, and no sign that the fingers had ever worn a ring.

The Blessed Mother knelt before me and kissed my bare hands. Suddenly, a ring appeared on my finger, and Elsslin writhed at my feet, her bright skin tortured by the flames of purgatory. In one arm, she held our child, who was equally punished in the fire in spite of his innocence. Elsslin held out her other arm toward me, begging me to lift her out of their misery. There was no mistaking the choice.

My mind returned to our bedroom, and I felt the Glorious Virgin's frozen gaze judge me again.

"If you wish my love, you'll get out of this bed at once and come with me before daybreak. Hurry up, get dressed, and leave this house! Go!"

This time, I didn't even shout. The fear spurred me to throw off the covers and find my clothes. I put my leggings on in the moonlight, left my false ring on the windowsill, and stepped into my boots, not daring to look on Elsslin, and certainly not to say anything to her. I hoped she understood that this way, I was saving us both unbearable torment.

I pulled my tunic over my head as I dashed out the door with no idea where I was headed. My only thought was to follow the Spiritual Queen's orders as fast as I could. I hurried through the empty streets while my neighbors slept in their houses, oblivious to the pressure only I felt to get out. I passed the tables with the vestiges of our wedding banquet still left to clean—empty tureens, deflated wineskins, platters piled high with bones.

For more than a month, I wandered through the forest, where thoughts of the Glorious Virgin kept me from feeling hunger or cold. I caught a few fish, foraged for edible shrubs and leaves, avoided the roads, and slept under branches so no bears or wildcats would find me.

When my clothes drooped on me the way a banner hangs on a pole, I found the hermitage on the other side of the forest. The four monks looked at me and took me in immediately out of charity. When I'd had some porridge and ale and found a bit of strength, I told them I wanted to serve St. Mary for the rest of my life.

And so I have, through work and prayer. When my time comes, I have no doubt she will come for me again, and this time take me with her to Paradise.

The Unwary Host

Cantiga 67

Carrión de los Condes, Spain, thirteenth century

This afternoon, the hostel was nearly complete. The plasterers had finished their work, and twelve bed frames languished in my barn. I dared not have them brought inside because I hadn't found anyone who would make and hang the door. Two masons were framing the hearth, and I stood in the empty doorframe, wondering whether I should make a trip into town to buy cookpots and ask if anyone knew where I could find good woodworkers who would dare to hang the door. I pay handsomely, after all.

But perhaps word was abroad about my standards. I only expect the work to be worth what I pay. We can't have the door of the free hostel for pilgrims rotting through or falling off its hinges within the year. I want this place to welcome travelers for a long time to come.

I turned inside the hostel to tell the masons where I was going, but before I said anything, someone cleared his throat behind me.

Strange. I hadn't noticed anyone nearby.

I turned back around to see a young man with a pleasant face. His red velvet tunic, though simple, made his status clear. The patent leather of his pointed shoes was impeccably clean there amid the soil of the construction site.

"Are you Don Filadelfo?" His voice rang out crystalline and resonated in the empty chamber behind me.

"I am. And you are?"

"My name is Cresconio." He bowed deeply, sweeping the hem of his tunic to the height of the leather purse at his waist. His movements flowed with the grace of an oriental magnate, and I was fascinated; however, I had the presence of mind to shake his hand in a brotherly fashion when he stood up.

"You are the good Christian they talk about for miles around," he continued, "who gives all he acquires to the Church because he loves charity above all?"

I laughed off his flattery. "I don't know what they say of me, but it is true I love doing good works. Are you come to be my salaried employee? I always welcome more help with so many projects, but I'll have to put you to a test first."

"What do you wish, sir? Give me your command."

"At this very moment, I was thinking of going to town to seek someone who can make and hang the front door to my hostel here, so I can start putting furniture inside and find an innkeeper and a cook."

Cresconio eyed the door frame behind me. "Go into town, sir, but do not worry about finding a workman. I shall take care of this for you."

I considered that there was nothing to steal inside the hostel, and the masons, a father and his son, wouldn't let this stranger do any harm to the building they had worked on with nearly as much devotion as I had. I let them know I was going to town, and that they should let Cresconio do what he would.

I had a mug of wine and a pleasant conversation with the tavernkeeper about the progress on the hostel. I didn't mention Cresconio's sudden appearance, but I did find out that there was no one who could build a good door and hang it well between here and León. I'm not sure I spent even an hour in town.

When I returned, I didn't expect to find Cresconio at the hostel at all. I thought he would be away looking for materials, or even have given up due to the difficulty of the task. I wouldn't have blamed him. But there he was, standing in front of the hostel, coolly nodding his head at the masons and a couple of children besides, who gawked and pointed at the door. Not the empty doorway, but a very fine door. It looked made of durable oak and rested perfectly straight on its golden hinges. The floral motifs in its four corners looked as if they would've taken months to carve.

"How did this come about?" I asked the masons.

The father crossed himself. "I don't know. Suddenly the light from the doorway was blocked, so we looked up from our work. The door was just there. My son dared to open it, and felt how solid it is, that it's truly here and not some phantasm. We came outside, and here's this fellow, arms folded, self-satisfied, and not saying a word to us."

I looked at Cresconio, who dropped to one knee before me. "My lord, take me for your servant, and I shall gladly do service for the poor, for I see that you are doing worthy deeds. And I shall even donate my service to you."

I examined his noble features and his extraordinary door.

"That's very generous. If I don't pay you a salary, I can provide all the more meat, fish, and bread to this hostel."

"Don Filadelfo, won't you even ask him where he got the door?" the stonemason asked.

"I come from a family of woodworkers," Cresconio said to me.

I considered that I might be in the presence of St. Joseph himself or someone sent by him. "It seems to me you understand my mission of charity and act in good faith. I'll take you for my personal squire."

The good fellow followed me home, and I arranged for a bed in the room next to mine. I'm thrilled to be able to take the beds and kitchen items to the hostel tomorrow. It's only right that people should be going on pilgrimage in springtime!

One thing is bothering me about the door. It really should have AVE MARIA carved into the front at eye level. I'll see if it can be done.

In Carrión, on the twenty-fifth of March.
In the name of the Glorious Virgin,
Queen of Mercy. Amen.

The hostel has been up and running for a week now, and already word is going around among pilgrims that it's a comfortable place to stay. Travelers throw their hands up in astonishment when they realize it's free of charge. If I'm not there, my innkeeper tells them about my devotion to St. Mary, that I want to make sure her pilgrims arrive safely to her shrine. We'll soon be at full capacity daily, with so much good springtime weather. Soon the rose bushes we've planted at the front of the garden will bloom. Everyone will see the Glorious Queen's flowers, then read the AVE MARIA I had one of the woodworking apprentices carve on the door, and they'll know they're in the right place.

This morning, Cresconio came to me, as usual, while I breakfasted. He stood at attention at the table, not even glancing at the food. "The hostel is a great success, sir. Anyone would judge that you are due for some leisure. Will you consider that your work is done, at least for the day?"

"There's always more charity I can do, more generosity to show. Now that the hostel is finished, I'm thinking of approaching the church about renovating the nave. It's quite sturdy, but a bit out of fashion."

"Such plans will take months, sir. You needn't be in any hurry to start." He took a few paces along the table to face me from his standing position. His blue eyes projected an icy calm. "This is a splendid moment to go into the mountains. I know a place with excellent hunting. We could bring back plenty of fox pelts. Or rabbits and pheasants for the hostel."

Game for the hostel! I set down the bread I had nearly finished. "I haven't been to the mountains for nearly a year," I said, standing. "You anticipate my every need. We'll go right now."

"Wonderful, sir. I shall prepare the horses, and I shall personally take you to the best spot I have visited in previous years."

The path up the mountain was steep and twisting. I'd certainly never visited there before. But Cresconio never hesitated, never needed to look back to see whether I followed his sure steps. I trusted he would bring us to a fine day of hunting.

We stopped in a clearing surrounded by pine forest high above the valley. Songbirds crossed the sunny sky with its last tinges of winter. Cresconio dismounted.

"Rabbits hide in these bushes, sir. I shall scare them out for you." He found a large switch on the ground and rattled it in the brush, making a tremendous clatter.

I seized my lance from its holder, thinking I might be able

to clip a hare as it bounded by. But no rabbits were in that clearing. The noise attracted something much bigger. An enormous brown form lurched between the bushes, its claws digging into the soft ground, its ears twitching, huffing. A bear.

I'm no fool. I stayed still, my heart pounding in my ears, one hand on my horse's neck to keep him calm, holding my breath a little. My other hand sweated against the polished wood of the lance. The bear's shaggy coat hung loosely on his thin frame. He was fresh out of hibernation. Hungry. But my horse and I were larger than he, and a bear in such weak condition wouldn't dare to take on such large prey.

I slowly turned my head toward Cresconio to make sure he was keeping as still as I, but his horse was alone, prancing about, looking for a way through the thick underbrush. Cresconio wasn't there.

The bear growled, taking a step toward the lone horse. Then his movements changed. He seemed to come into a new power, and ran toward me as if on a mission.

"St. Mary, save me!" I cried.

The bear stood to his full height, his claws and daggerlike teeth even with my horse's muzzle. My horse reared.

As if guided by a celestial hand, I tilted with the horse, and the point of my lance entered the bear's gut. My horse kicked at the bear, and it fell backward, taking my lance with it.

The bear must've died immediately, but I sat astride my horse, staring at it, waiting to understand what had happened.

Movement caught my eye off to the side, and I looked to see that though his horse had long before found a way out of the clearing, Cresconio stood in exactly the spot where he'd been before the bear appeared.

"Where did you go?" I shouted. "You're meant to guide me safely through these mountains!"

"I have been here all the time, sir," he said with detached coolness. "Did you not see me waving this stick? I tried to draw the bear away from you."

Suddenly, in my mind's eye, I remembered him exactly as he said, behind the bear, flailing his arms and shouting. I shook my head. In spite of all that, the bear had chosen to attack me and my horse, even though we were still and silent.

"St. Mary is truly watching over me." I crossed myself, kissed my amulet, and regarded the white clouds in the sky above us.

"Yes." Cresconio dropped the stick and clapped his hands. "Sir, you will bring a much bigger prize than I anticipated to the hostel. I shall fetch my horse, and we can find a way to balance the weight on his saddle."

He ducked through the bushes, leaving me to dismount unsteadily and regard the bear close up. The animal looked vastly smaller than it had when it attacked, and given its post-hibernation state, I doubted there was much meat on the bones.

In the end, it was as Cresconio said. We brought the carcass to the hostel, and the cooks butchered it and roasted it outside. The pilgrims staying at the hostel played instruments and danced, and a few townspeople joined the party. At the end of the evening, we held hands and sang Ave Maris Stella around the dying embers. I returned home alone, however. I looked in Cresconio's room, and he was already sleeping soundly in his clothes, without a blanket. I guessed his efforts had tired him, and decided I wouldn't reprimand his going to bed without being dismissed.

> In Carrión, on the twenty-first of April.
> In the name of the Glorious Virgin,
> Queen of Mercy. Amen.

I have no complaint about Cresconio, especially given that he works for free. Almost the only thing he ever says to me is, "What do you wish, sir? Give me your command." His work is exemplary, usually just as miraculous as the door his first day.

Yesterday I had many of the noble families of the region to a dinner that lasted well into the night. At the end of the evening, the only servant still awake was Cresconio. He had welcomed the guests with special attention in the afternoon and never ceased to see to their wishes with the same assiduousness he always carried out mine. I would've understood if he'd turned in with the rest, but he stayed at my side, more loyal than any dog.

There must've been hundreds of beeswax candles illuminating the great hall, along the table, in the corners on tall candelabras, lining the shuttered windows, so that my guests wouldn't stumble in the dark. By the time the guests were ready to retire to the special lodgings we'd prepared for them in the outbuildings, the candles were burnt to stubs.

But I didn't want to chance a tragedy, so I asked Cresconio to snuff them all out. I was sure the task would take an hour or longer, and intended to return to the hall and help him after I bade good night to the guests. The formalities didn't take long, as everyone was tired. I threw the bolt in the main house door and turned, only to narrowly avoid knocking Cresconio down.

"What's wrong?" I asked. I couldn't imagine what he was doing at the front of the house.

"I have finished, sir. What else do you wish?"

As quickly as I could without blowing out the candle I carried, I returned to the great hall. It was dark. There was no way to tell where the room ended in the deep blackness.

I remained speechless. "How did you do it so quickly?" I said at last.

"Any burden would be light if it were in service to you, sir."

And I remember how he tried to save me from the bear, giving thanks to St. Mary. I only hope I can serve her as well as Cresconio serves me.

But during Holy Week, he left without telling me where he was going, and only returned the evening of Easter Monday. I suppose it's right that he should be with whatever family he has during those important celebrations, but he's so well mannered in all else. Why didn't he say something before he left?

Although he always seems clean, he doesn't wash with anyone else in the household. Today I learned where he might be washing, and it's just as well he keeps apart from us.

He was helping me bring a cartload of wineskins to the hostel. He lifted the wineskins out of the cart by twos and laid them in front of the door. I took them from there, and the cooks helped me retrieve and store them when they saw what I had. I finished to find Cresconio standing idle at the lip of the empty cart, scratching his head.

When he heard me, he turned and stood crisply to offer me his usual, "What do you wish, sir?"

I had the intention to tell him to get in the cart, and I would mount the horse, and we would return to my house together. But an enormous white louse crawled from his hairline, circled his ear, and hid itself again in that hair that had seemed so well cared for. I lost the power of speech with my astonishment.

"I am sorry you saw that, sir. I have been trying to remedy the problem by washing in the river rather than in the baths, but the cure is long in coming."

"Have you been to see a physician or a woman who makes poultices and tisanes?"

"My physician is the one who told me to bathe in the river."

"Well, the best cure is surely to pray to St. Mary. No sickness is beyond the Glorious Queen's power." I contemplated the AVE MARIA in the door.

If he replied, I didn't hear it. When I looked back at him, he had climbed into the cart in his customary anticipation of my wishes. Given how well he takes care of every task I set to him, I have no concerns that he'll recover from this incident of uncleanliness quickly.

In Carrión, on the twenty-fifth of April.
In the name of the Glorious Virgin,
Queen of Mercy. Amen.

No day after that has Cresconio shown any crawling thing on him. I don't know how he solved his problem, and only hope I never need think about it again.

I write today about something that could have been unfortunate. Cresconio came to me at breakfast, asking what I wished. The fine weather and smooth operations at the hostel provided a new answer.

"Do you fish, Cresconio?"

His eyes darkened for an instant. "No, sir. I have not had the privilege of anyone teaching me to fish. Do you desire to go fishing?"

"I do. You'll come with me, and in helping me, you'll learn everything you need to know."

He stayed quiet, perhaps apprehensive that he wouldn't be able to help me with tasks he'd never done before. When we arrived at the riverbank, and he caught sight of my boat tied to its pole, his expression lightened.

"Would you have me row, sir?"

"Can you row? That would be very fine, Cresconio." If he took care of moving us along the river, I could attend to the nets and make a better catch.

I heaved the nets into the boat and stepped in. I heard Cresconio working with the rope, untying the boat behind me, but didn't think to check that he understood how it was done. Suddenly, I felt a great push. The boat lurched forward as if it had been launched. I nearly lost my balance and toppled into the river.

I looked behind me to see Cresconio standing on the riverbank, the rope in his hand, watching the boat with a frozen expression.

The river's current quickened, and the boat floated away from my employee faster and faster. He couldn't have reached me if he tried. I thought I would flow with the river out to sea or be bashed upon rocks.

I passed by a thorny bush and thought to catch it in a fishing net and stop the boat's inevitable deadly progress. But the net slipped out of my hands as if I had never held onto one before and veiled the bush like a nun.

"St. Mary, Queen of Heaven, help me!" I cried.

The river slowed. The current behaved irregularly, creating eddies. One after the other, these whirlpools pushed the boat into a small inlet. The boat docked gently into the muddy bank, and I stepped out onto a grassy area as if it had been my intention all along. I grasped the net to my heart and fell to my knees, offering thanks to my savior with a ragged Gaude Virgo.

Cresconio didn't approach me until I'd finished singing.

"You are all right then, sir," he said.

"No thanks to you," I said standing. "Why did you push the boat off like that? Why didn't you join me in the boat?"

"I tried, sir, but the boat escaped me. I am not accustomed to such things and must have been clumsy."

As soon as he said it, it was as if I had witnessed it myself. Clearly, he was even more inept than he'd let on.

"Well, I guess we won't take you on any more fishing trips until someone has shown you how to board a boat."

We took no fish home, but we were able to salvage the net I'd thrown at the thorn bush. I'd thought it would be full of rips and snags, but I found it as whole as the day it was made.

In Carrión, on the fifth of May.

In the name of the Glorious Virgin,

Queen of Mercy. Amen.

Summer has passed with its warmth and sunshine, and by the Blessed Virgin's mercy, I and all in my house are well. I visited the building site at the church a few times. Once while observing the placement of the new foundations from above, I nearly fell off a ladder when someone ran into it. Luckily, there was an image of the Mother of God below the ladder, too, and she stabilized it.

We'd been preparing for Bishop Simón's visit for months. The saintly bishop of our diocese and his household would break bread with me and mine and then sing a mass in honor of St. Gregory's day. Cresconio had been as faithful as usual, always asking me what I wished. But yesterday morning, I felt as if I were missing my right arm, because Cresconio was nowhere to be found.

I saw to the cleaning, including the beating of the tapestries, the arrangement of the furniture, the cooking, the table setting, the lighting, everything, myself, when what I could really have used was Cresconio's swiftness and perfection. I had no time to check on him; I barely knew who I was by the time the bishop arrived. Luckily, another servant noticed I'd sweated through my tunic and laid another out for me.

I slipped the new tunic over my head and was cinching the belt when a maid knocked on my chamber door.

"He's here! Come and meet Bishop Simón!"

I hurried to the reception area at the front door, expecting to see a retinue of servants, enough to fill up my carefully laid table twice over, complete with horses, colorful standards, and even a litter for the bishop to ride in. I hadn't met him yet, but everything I'd heard about his power and nobility suggested I was to be honored with the arrival of a prince of the Church.

But there was no page, servant, litter, pendant, or even a horse to be seen. The bishop arrived on foot with a simple walking staff. His cape in Mary's color, bright blue, flowed with a silkiness that indicated its high quality, but it was unadorned.

"Who's coming here?" asked the maid who waited at my side. "He looks like a merchant from the city."

"It's the bishop," I replied, hardly believing it myself. But no one could wear the white triangle miter, as simple as it was, except the bishop.

"Don Filadelfo," he said, taking me into his arms. "I've long wanted to meet you. The fame of your charity extends throughout the land."

I felt humbled receiving the admiration of someone so unexpectedly humble himself. "You honor me too much, Your Excellency." I showed him inside.

"Nonsense. At the cathedral, they've told me about your pilgrims' hostel, how well they eat and sleep there, and that it's completely free of charge. And they say you've also started work on enlarging your parish church."

"It's dedicated to St. Mary. I couldn't bear such a small nave as a house for the Queen of Heaven."

We arrived in the great hall, and Bishop Simón smiled and

took the hand of every servant who wished it. There were scores of empty seats and place settings because of the crowd of attendants I'd expected, but he chose to sit next to me.

I was so honored to dine with this holy man that I didn't notice how long it took to get the first course served. The bishop didn't complain. He continued to converse pleasantly. But when I noticed the angle of the sunlight coming through the window change between the first and second courses, I couldn't understand the delay. There weren't even half the people we'd been expecting at the table. Cresconio would never have let this happen.

When the second course finally arrived, I asked the server, "Where is Cresconio? I haven't seen him all day."

He answered while carefully ladling the bishop's broth into his bowl. "We looked for him this morning, sir, and found him in his bed. He says he's unwell, and he's stayed there all day."

"Today of all days," I said. "How strange." As the server bowed and moved along the table to the other guests, I wondered whether Cresconio's lice problem had returned and he was too ashamed to stand before the bishop.

"Who is abed?" asked Bishop Simón. "Perhaps I should visit him."

"I miss Cresconio now, Your Excellency, because my other servants do excellent work, but only Cresconio could serve us with the swiftness and grace I'd hoped to show you."

"This Cresconio is special, is he?"

"I might presume to say his work is miraculous. He hung the door at the hostel when no one else dared try, and so quickly, no one saw him do it. He snuffed out hundreds of candles across this great hall in the blink of an eye, he tried to save me from a bear and from floating away on the river current, and if I'd fallen off the ladder at the church, he says he would've caught me."

The bishop dropped his spoon. He regarded me with a furrowed brow. "And how long has this Cresconio worked for you?"

"Since the end of March. He appeared when I most needed him, and worked the miracle of the door, as I told Your Excellency. I hired him on the spot, and he's hardly left my side."

The bishop raised his hand and the server returned. "Bring this Cresconio to me," the bishop told him. "I wish to speak with him."

"Yes, Your Excellency." The server ran back to the kitchen.

"He's an exemplary servant," I assured Bishop Simón.

"I'm certain he is."

We waited. The bishop didn't pick up his spoon again. A maid brought a burning candle into the great hall and used it to light more so we wouldn't be overtaken by the dark.

When Cresconio finally arrived, he struggled between the two servants who obliged him to walk, gripping his arms.

"He resisted, Your Excellency," said one servant.

"We couldn't convince him to come," said the other.

Cresconio didn't seem ill, although his face was ashen. He stood before the bishop as if he could stand nowhere else and hung his head. He didn't acknowledge me, much less ask me what I wished.

"Don Filadelfo," Bishop Simón said, crossing himself, "God loves you, have no doubt. If you listen for but a while, I'll show you how you've avoided being led astray by the Devil and his treacheries."

Several guests gasped. A lady screamed.

"The Devil?" I yelped.

All the light in the room shone upon the bishop. He stood, hands on the table, and suddenly towered over Cresconio and the rest of us. "Tell me all that you have done, so that this company may learn of your misdeeds. I command you by the power of Jesus Christ, who is God in Trinity, that you withhold nothing."

Cresconio pursed his lips, willing himself not to speak. He turned away from the table, bending over, but was snapped back to face us by a celestial hand. Finally, his mouth opened.

"I am a demon sent by Lucifer to kill this man unconfessed and drag his soul to Hell. I dressed myself in the body of a handsome knight, who left it behind after a battle."

His tunic lifted under its own power, revealing an open wound that stretched from one side to the other over the stomach. Things oozed in the candlelight, and I looked away to see that though we heard the words, the mouth wasn't moving. The voice came from much deeper within the body and echoed through empty chambers.

"I gained this man's confidence doing efficient work for him. Then I sent a hungry bear to kill him. I pushed his boat in the hope that it would be smashed upon the rocks in the river current I quickened. I pushed him off a ladder. I continued in my mission to claim his soul because Lucifer's greed and cruelty know no bounds. But every day, this man says a prayer to the Mother of Jesus, and calls on her when he is in trouble. When he said these prayers, I could not harm him."

The fine clothing sank inward for lack of a frame to rest on. A black form, much darker than any earthly shadow, floated out of the mouth toward some of my guests. They ducked out of the way, and the form dissipated through the open window. The handsome body of the man I had known as Cresconio crumpled to the floor with a thud.

Shaking, I looked at Bishop Simón. Together, we brought a candle to inspect the corpse. The skin was desiccated, yellow and brown in patches, and the face was sunken over the skull beneath a hairless scalp. If anyone screamed, I didn't hear it.

"What happened wasn't this man's fault," the bishop said. "He gave his life in battle and we must hold vigil."

Bishop Simón was the only one who dared to touch the corpse to lay it out under a veil. In the morning, I helped dig the grave, and Bishop Simón granted the knight, whose name we never knew, the benefit of all his blessings. As he left, he gave a special blessing to me, although we agreed I already enjoy St. Mary's protection.

> In Carrión, on the fourth of September.
> Praise the name of the Glorious Virgin,
> Queen of Mercy! With her power, she
> always defends her own against
> the Devil and his malice. Amen.

The Lamb and the Wolf

Cantiga 147

Rocamadour, France, thirteenth century

There I was, without a soul in the world to give a care for me except the Glorious Queen up on her throne in Heaven. I never could catch a husband, but at least I looked after my parents here below the mountain and had the family home from them when they passed on. All I'd ever wanted since I was a young girl, when I caught sight of the shepherds herding their flocks up and down the hills, was a little sheep of my own who would grow soft wool I could spin into cloth. I never knew how to act on that desire while my parents were alive.

Finding myself alone with a few chickens in the yard, I took to visiting St. Mary's sanctuary at the top of the rock. The climb cleared my head, and one day as I knelt before the image of Our Lady, she planted an idea that grew without any effort of my own. I thanked her as best I could and lit a candle, then hurried back down to knock on the doors in my street.

I roused all my neighbors from their tasks, some of them protesting greatly, and gathered them in the shepherds' hermitage, which was easier to get to than Mary's shrine. Right there on the porch, I stood before my neighbors, and I must've had the Holy Spirit about me, because they paid attention to me as none ever had before.

"Friends," I said, "we all live on the same street, and we all have at least one chicken each. We all pay our taxes and eat more or less every day, but there's little left at the end of the year to put a new roof on, or for those of you lucky enough to have children, to put shoes on their little feet."

Behind the rest of the adults, the children of our street chased each other around the one pitiable woman who'd been tasked with watching them during the meeting. Most of them had something decent on their feet, but my audience nodded and grumbled their agreement.

"Some days our chickens lay, and some days they don't. But today I thought, we don't have to rely on their whims for our survival. If we put all of our chickens together into one big coop, we can let each one take a fair share of the eggs. If we set it up right with good roosters, in no time at all, we'll have enough to sell at a profit."

Sighs and whispering. They couldn't imagine it yet.

"Albert and Matilde have the biggest yard," I said, signaling to the couple whose children had moved to other streets and cities long ago. "We could put all the chickens we have now and multiply them there and still have room to spare."

"We used to have goats," said Matilde.

The murmuring increased. I sensed that they thought it might work. "We can adapt the fence into a coop ourselves. We can take turns feeding them. And Jacques can tie one of his dogs to either side of the coop to keep the cats away."

"Only at night," said Jacques. "I might need them during the day."

Simone shouted from the back. "What if a wolf comes?"

"My dogs can take any wolf, any day," said Jacques, as I'd hoped.

"Or a wild boar?" said Julien.

"A wild boar would crash into a lot of other things on our street before the chicken coop, and he'd be loud enough that we could hear him coming and help," I said. "So it's agreed?"

"But who decides who gets how many eggs?" Rafael folded his arms over his chest skeptically. "And who feeds the chickens when? And if we sell chickens or roosters, who gets the money? It has to be fair."

I looked into the faces of all my neighbors, trying to guess who was the most evenhanded. I'd imagined myself doing the counting on this enterprise. It was my project, after all, given to me by St. Mary herself. But it would be better to assign the responsibility to someone who had nothing to do with me.

Thérèse saved me from hesitation. "Pierre's helped out the tax collectors when they come through here for years." She punched his shoulder. "And the fact that he's not volunteering means he's honest."

I applauded the nomination. "Who agrees to set up the community chicken coop under these conditions, in Albert and Matilde's yard, with Jacques's dogs, and Pierre doing the accounting? Show of hands."

Many hands went straight into the air. A few followed after mumbling, "Why not?" The last ones were cajoled with, "Oh, go on, give it a try."

"If it doesn't seem to be working, we can stop any time," I said, my hand raised in oath. "May St. Mary bless our endeavor."

It was never necessary to dismantle the community chicken coop because it worked from the start. I helped Albert and some of the other men set up the fencing the next day, and on Sunday after mass at Our Lady's church, we carried our chickens in our arms or in sacks, or let the children run around herding them in a strange procession to their new home.

We loosed the roosters in the street and saved five of the least warriorlike from the others, setting apart six to eight chickens for each of them. With their gentler natures, I knew that many chickens should be enough to keep them too busy to fight each other. Over the course of several weeks, I searched out new flocks for the other roosters in neighboring streets and paid the owners 90 percent of what I received for them.

Soon enough, the coop began producing more eggs than we could consume. I decided which ones we should let hatch to then sell the chicken or rooster, and which ones we should sell as eggs. It seemed I was always going to the market and selling out of everything I'd brought. The money flowed to us like a spring brook, slowly growing into a stream. The steady success convinced my neighbors to trust me, and our street began having our own feasts on saints' days. On other days, someone always came to my house to chat, usually leaving vegetables, fish, or sweets.

I planted as many stalks of wheat as I could fit into the area where my chickens had been, and in a couple of years, I hardly even had to pay for my daily bread.

As I have no children to clothe, and, St. Mary be praised, my house was as sound as the day my father laid the last stone, I waited until my friends left and stashed my money in the bench next to the table with an eye to saving enough to one day buy my little sheep. When the livestock market came to Rocamadour, I was ready.

I walked to the fairground by myself, a lady in control of her own humble household. I knew the way well, as I'd made my way to the fair every year to get an idea of the offerings. I probably looked much poorer than I was, with my mended clothes and worn shoe soles. My richness was hidden under my overskirt, weighing down my purse, even though I'd been exchanging small coins for more valuable ones for easier transport. I huffed through the fields to the riotous market. I smelled it before it came into view.

Cattle in every color lowed behind gates, goats kicked and butted each other in pens, and hogs squealed as they were loaded off carts and into stalls. But I didn't pause until I came to the sheep. Some still wore their bells, and most bleated mournfully. In that chaos, I felt much more at home. As I cupped the purse and felt the cold, hard weight of the coins, I'd never felt freer in my life. I strolled, feigning disinterest even as I inspected each animal in each pen from afar. I didn't dare go close enough for the sellers to look at me in case I forgot myself and let my excitement show.

None of the bleating animals were for me. Their long faces and black legs were the kind I'd seen all my life, but I didn't feel a stirring, no desire to lay out my coins or take any of them from this place.

Until I came to the pen with the vendor I'd never met before. He seemed to have come a long way, with his wide-brimmed hat and strangely turned shoes. They looked comfortable, but what I noticed was that his sheep were as different as he was. Their short coats were a lighter gray color, and they milled about the pen gracefully, not bumping into and climbing over each other like in the rest of the pens. Even their bleats had a richer, less shrill tone. One little sheep didn't make any sound at all, and before I knew it, my hands were on top of the fencing as I irresistibly tried to get a closer look. I just managed to keep myself from vaulting over the gate.

The seller sidled right up to me. "If they look different to you, it's because they're the best sheep you've ever seen." His accent was odd, too. "I've brought them myself all the way from Spain."

"Wherever that is, it's not close by," I said, trying to look skeptical. "You'll have worn them out with all that travel."

"Oh, no," said the vendor. "They're traveling sheep. They move great distances every year all over Spain. This is only a little farther than usual. Look at their condition. You won't see a hardier flock at this whole fair."

I couldn't deny it. I dared not look at him. "I'm only interested in buying one sheep."

"Just one?" It was as if no one had ever asked for that number before.

"That one," I said pointing. "In the middle, the quiet one."

"She's just past a year old. That's all the wool she's ever grown, but next year, you'll be able to get enough off her for several garments." He eyed me, guessing what I wanted. "And you'll be able to charge a lot for her wool. No one in your village will have anything like it."

"May I feel it?" I asked, reaching toward her. She saw my hand and wove through stamping feet and flicking tails, right up to the fence. The vendor said something, but it hardly mattered because up close, her eyes invited me to scratch her ears. Then my hand went to her fuzzy back. The seller was right. The fibers were still short, but strong, and my fingers combed through them as through freshly churned cream, the smoothest, softest wool I'd ever touched. She responded by wriggling and reaching up to try and kiss my other hand.

I laughed. I was unable to resist the visions of shearing and working her wool into tunics and capes to sell. What a pleasure it would be. "How much?"

"Fifteen *sous*," said the vendor.

I gasped. That price would leave me with just a few small coins, and I would have to give those to a shepherd, since I had no way to take care of the sheep myself. My bench would be empty until I could start over again with the eggs.

"I could give you a discount if you bought more."

I ignored that impossible statement. "What do you think, little one?" I asked the sheep. "Has the Queen of Heaven sent you to me?"

She stamped her legs and batted her eyelashes as if to say yes, though she didn't use her voice.

"This will be my ruin," I murmured, my hand fumbling between my skirts in the purse. Shakily, I pulled out all the coins I'd brought. "Fifteen *sous*."

The vendor lifted them from my hand, and I exhaled, but I wasn't sure if it was with relief or distress. He stowed my life savings in a chest in the back of his cart, then stepped into the pen and lifted my sheep over the fence, directly into my arms.

"I'll see you next year when you want to increase your flock," he said.

I set my sheep down because I wasn't that much bigger, and without the weight of the coins, I thought I might topple over. "I just gave you all my money. I don't have more to increase my flock."

"Oh, you will, come shearing time," he replied with a wink.

"Whatever you say," I whispered, though I felt certain I'd made the right decision. My little sheep followed me closely all the way home, her hooves tapping a sprightly beat in my ears.

I was humming along as I entered my house and held the door until my little sheep decided to join me.

She looked so lovely between the table and the fireplace, peering curiously at everything, putting her mouth to the table edge and nudging the bench. Then she bleated for the first time. It was gentle, high, and sweet, like when the choir imitates angels during Mary's masses. And I couldn't be sure, but it sounded like "*Maman*."

All that work, all those savings, never being the mother of any child, had led to becoming the mother of a little sheep? I liked the idea. I bent to kiss her forehead and gave her ears a good scratch. I hesitated to open the bench and take out the paltry rest of my savings that were left to me from four years of ideas, deals, and hard work, to pay the shepherd.

But no, as sweet as she was, she couldn't sleep with me in my bed or stay home when I went to sell at market. She needed to be with a flock and eat in the fields. So I filled my purse again and opened the door so I could entrust my little sheep to the shepherd, who lived halfway out of town.

"Here is my dear little sheep, and here are the coins I promised you," I said when he stuck his head out between the door and the frame.

He snatched up the coins and counted them. I wanted to march back home with my sheep, but I had little choice. "You'll mark her with paint or give her a bell so you always know she's mine?"

"Sure," he grunted.

I knelt and nuzzled her and she kissed the palm of my hand. "And your dogs will protect her all the time and make sure no wolf ever gets near?"

"Yup." He pulled my sheep by the ear toward the barn. She didn't protest, but tried to twist back and look at me.

"And you'll make sure the other sheep accept her?" I tried. "She's a bit different."

"Sure thing."

"I'll be back at shearing time."

He didn't bother to answer that time. He'd already disappeared into the barn with my little sheep. I stood there for a few minutes, but he didn't come back out, and I supposed there was nothing left to do. I went back home with no weight in my purse and no hoofbeats at my side.

Over those long months, my empty house seemed to ask, over and over, whether this was really what I had worked so hard and so long for. I busied myself taking more turns feeding the chickens, digging up more stones in my yard to make room for more wheat, and driving harder bargains when I sold at market every week. After all, everyone knew ours were the best, both the chickens and the eggs. When I helped Thérèse cut and sew, she gave me some percentage of her earnings. But when I'd mended all my clothes and swept the house so clean not even a mouse could live there, visions of my little sheep's deep brown eyes plagued me. I imagined her in the fields, running and playing and eating her fill, far from me. At times like that, the only cure was to head up the mountain and kneel before the Glorious Virgin. Her placid face and slim black hand raised in blessing calmed my heart and saved my soul from desperation many a time.

I couldn't save much money, what with the heavy rains in the autumn calling for a roof repair and buying more chickens for a bigger share in the poultry business. I reckoned I needed the cash I could get from my sheep's wool to stretch through the next month before my spring and summer profits came in. If I could earn enough for that, along with the gratification of finally having a sheep and fine wool to sell, I would consider myself satisfied.

I was so looking forward to seeing my dear little sheep again that I would've walked through snow banks as tall as trees without complaint. But as it happened, it was one of those pre-spring mornings, bright but cold on the skin. The smell of new growths that would later become flowers accompanied me along the path out of town to the shepherd's house. I turned a corner and the street opened out into hills where my sheep must've spent the summer. The sun rose over the ridge and cast its blessing rays over the landscape.

I knocked on the shepherd's door with a wide smile. What seemed like ages later, he opened the door in his undershirt, rubbing his eyes. "Yes?"

My smile was long gone by then. "It's shearing time. I'm here for my Spanish sheep."

"That was the little one that hardly ever made a noise?"

"The one I brought to you nearly a year ago."

"Very light gray wool, soft to the touch?"

I think of myself as patient, but this shepherd was testing me to the breaking point. "That's her. Where is she?"

"The wolf ate it."

"What? What wolf? I never heard about any wolf. I told you to keep my sheep safe from wolves!"

"The fierce bastard murdered one of my dogs and half my flock, and your little sheep was one of the first to go."

This day was supposed to be the best day, full of joy, not sorrow, and there I was, weeping. "Why didn't you tell me?"

"I got a whole flock to take care of. It was just one sheep out of hundreds."

"But she's my only sheep." My one desire, my only love, the

place where all my hope lay. It simply couldn't be true. I wiped my tears. "You're lying." St. Mary wouldn't let my sheep come to this end, not after these years of labor and care, not after I followed her instructions to get the chicken coop started.

My skin felt like it was on fire, all the way to my scalp. I turned away from the shepherd in righteous rage and stormed toward his barn. Halfway there, I dropped to my knees and raised my hands to the sky.

"Oh, Glorious Lady, let me have my sheep. It's in your power."

I was determined to stay there, my arms twinging, pebbles and rocks digging into my knees even through my skirts, and wait until St. Mary was able to change the shepherd's mind or sent my sheep trotting back to me all by herself.

I didn't have to wait long.

From out of the barn, high and sweet, I heard my little sheep call to me like a minstrel's flute. She said, "*Maman*," again, or perhaps it was something more like, "Here I am."

I stood as fast as I was able, stifling groans, and took the time to brush off my skirt, deliberately not looking at the shepherd, whose guilty gaze I felt on me like a plagued breeze. I threw open the barn door, and it was full of noisy animals that didn't want to leave the warmth of their winter lodgings. I hadn't heard any of them from outside. My sheep was in the back, still calling to me over the din.

I pressed my hands together in thanks to the Glorious Queen, then waded through the other animals and ran my fingers through the luxuriously long wool of my own dear sheep. The shepherd's lie couldn't have been more exaggerated. Not only was she not eaten by a wolf, but her eyes and coat shone like glimmers on the river in the afternoon. I couldn't have picked her up, because she'd nearly doubled in size, but we pushed through the animals together, and I slammed the barn door shut behind us.

The shepherd was staring at me and my soft, wooly sheep. I thought about demanding back the coins I'd given him, but I was too filled with gratitude to Our Lady of Rocamadour. After all, my sheep was back in my care in great condition, so I left him to feel his guilt over trying to steal my life's work from me.

"It looks like it's you and me, after all, little one," I said even as I listened to the hoofbeats beside me. My mind raced: Where could my little sheep live? What would she eat? Which of my dull, broken knives could I shear her with? I wanted to avoid harming her, because she was adorable, and because I felt she partly belonged to St. Mary. It wouldn't do to damage the belongings of the Queen of Heaven.

Feeling the warming sunrays on my back, I thought perhaps Thérèse's scissors for cutting cloth would do the job. Instead of going home, I went straight to my friend's door. My little sheep nudged my legs and nearly knocked me over.

"Yes, it's exciting, isn't it? I'm going to cut that heavy coat off you, and you'll be cool enough to run about in a field, somewhere…"

Thérèse came to the door as the alarm took over my face. Where could my little sheep live? She couldn't go back to that crooked shepherd.

One thing at a time.

"Good day, Thérèse. This is my pride and joy, my little sheep. May I borrow your scissors to shear her?"

My friend ducked back into the house and emerged with the scissors and a folded sheet. "You can do it right here and gather the wool in this linen. But why didn't the shepherd do the shearing and give you the wool?"

"That underhanded son of Satan tried to hide my sheep from me and said a wolf ate her. But I knew he was lying, so I called on St. Mary to reveal my sheep, and she called out to me from where he'd hidden her. She hardly ever makes a sound, but she let me find her. You can bet I got out of there as fast as I could!"

"That sounds like a miracle to me," said Thérèse.

"Yes, it certainly was."

"Let me help you."

I held my sheep's face and kept her calm while Thérèse delicately snipped close to the skin, but never nicked the flesh. "Everything you said about this wool is true. It's the best I've ever seen. What are you planning to do with it?"

I brushed my sheep off and caressed her newly bare skin. We gathered the stray fluff into the sheet and folded it up into a pack. "All the saving I did to buy the sheep and then to pay the shepherd was with a mind to selling the wool. I'll give you some of my profits, since you helped."

"No, it's not that," said Thérèse. "I think this wool, which came to you by a miracle, belongs to Our Lady of Rocamadour. Don't you?"

If I gave the wool to the sanctuary, I would be left with a naked sheep shivering a little with the shock, a precious being for whom I couldn't provide a home or sustenance. How could my inspiration from St. Mary, the years of work it led to, and even a miraculous recovery of my sheep result in this? This couldn't be what the Glorious Queen intended for me, could it?

But I looked at my friend's anxious gaze, and watched other people come out of their homes to see what we were doing. They would all say the same thing. I couldn't sell the wool in good conscience. I owed everything to St. Mary. Since the wool was everything I had, I must take it to her.

Most of the residents of the street had gathered around us. I felt about as nervous as my little sheep, who tried to dart between the adults to avoid the children's grabbing hands. I raised my voice on faith alone.

"A miracle has occurred today. The Queen of Heaven granted this sheep to me when I thought she was lost. I'm going to take her wool and donate it to Mary's church at the top of the mountain. Who's coming with me?"

Thérèse embraced me and helped me heft the pack of wool onto my back. Several men in the crowd offered to carry it for me, but it was my wool for this little while longer, and I was taking it to its rightful owner myself. We progressed up the mountain slowly and noisily, with some songs, but mostly shouts and hurrahs. My little lamb tripped happily up the budding slope in the full sunlight.

Several of the monks came out of the buildings to see what the noise was about. I told one of them that my sheep was miraculous, so they went to fetch the abbot. I sank to my knees with the weight of the wool. My little lamb put her head in my lap, and I stroked her still soft head.

The abbot looked as if he had crowds of people waiting to tell him about miracles every day. He stood before me with his arms crossed over his crucifix.

"The shepherd told me my little sheep was dead," I explained. "But I cried out to St. Mary to return her to me, and so she made the sheep talk, letting me know where she was."

He nodded, high above me, looking as tall as the church tower, but seemed to be waiting for something else.

"And I've come to donate the wool to the Glorious Lady because it's hers, after all."

"This is the work of the Blessed Virgin, who always defends

us." He let us all into the church, even my little sheep. I made the sign of the cross on her because she couldn't do it herself.

I approached the altar and looked St. Mary in the eye. "Please accept this small token"—enormous prize I'd worked years for—"of my faithful devotion to you and gratitude for the beautiful miracle you granted me today." I placed the pack of wool before the altar and sat reverentially looking up at the Glorious Virgin, my sheep beside me, and the rest of my neighbors behind.

The rest of my neighbors except Thérèse, that is. After the short thanksgiving mass one of the priests gave, everyone was milling around, inspecting the candles at different altars and making a festival of it. I stood with my sheep, unsure of where to go or what to do.

My friend found me in the crowd, tugging at my sleeve. "Wonderful news! I've been talking with the prior, telling him how awful that shepherd was and how you don't have money to pay a different one to take your sheep now. He says your sheep can live here at the monastery. They have a little flock, and she'll fit right in."

I grasped Thérèse's hands in my excitement. "And I could come here and visit her sometimes?"

"Why not? He says they'll even let you do the shearing and take half the wool next year."

I wouldn't be left destitute after all. It truly was a miracle. I whooped for joy, and my little sheep cried, "*Maman! Maman!*" until we took her into the enclosure with the other sheep, and it was time for everyone to go home.

The Castle Across the Stream

Cantiga 185

Southern Spain, 1264

Auria awakened before dawn, before Jofré had stirred from his light baby slumber. Ever since her son's birth, misgivings about living with her husband at his frontier post had taken root in Auria, and sometimes they robbed her of sleep.

She slid out from under the covers slowly, so Sancho wouldn't feel the difference in weight on the bed strings and straw mattress. She lifted Jofré's swaddled bundle from the crib, seized the low-burning taper, and tiptoed into the castle's wide hallway.

"Let's beg the Virgin for peace," she murmured near her baby's soft cheek. "On the border and in my mind." She wound down the staircase, passing windows that looked onto the barracks roof in the courtyard, and on the other side, narrow slots intended for no one but archers to look out of. Auria's eye caught the glint of the rising sun on the river—barely more than a brook, really—that marked the beginning of the Kingdom of Granada.

She crossed the courtyard, giving a silent nod to the soldiers who were just waking. She entered another tower, and two flights up, she used the taper to illuminate the castle chapel. When she could make out the Last Supper tableau behind the altar, she set the taper down.

Still clasping Jofré to her breast, Auria knelt before the radiant image of St. Mary she had carried close to her all the way from the workshop in Segovia. It was on the corner of the street where she had grown up, married Sancho, and received King Alfonso's letter that had granted Chincoya Castle to Sancho and his heirs. She had been pregnant with Jofré when the letter arrived in Segovia, and it ought to have struck terror into her heart, but she hadn't known Chincoya was so far south. She hadn't known she would give birth with only a few startled foot soldiers for help, practically in the shadow of a Moorish castle across the stream. The letter had seemed to be the highest honor, a reward for Sancho's service to the king in the first years of his reign. But what king would grant his subject loneliness, hunger, and the constant threat of war?

"Forgive my ingratitude, Blessed Mother," Auria prayed. "Please intercede with your Son for us sinners. Please send us more soldiers to defend your castle, some women to help me honor you better, and more seed to plant and livestock to sustain us against the enemy. We've done all we can. We need your help now."

The seated figure was carved with miraculous detail in wood and painted with a blue veil, red tunic, and gold crown and shoes that showed under the hem. In her left arm, the Holy Mother cradled the infant Jesus in much the same way Auria held Jofré. The Virgin's right hand was raised in blessing, and often moved in the candlelight, but when the sun poured through the window, it stayed still. Auria crossed herself, then stood and gingerly brought Jofré's head under the Virgin's blessing hand. She kissed the gold shoes, then her baby's downy hair, and blew out the candles.

Jofré fussed as they passed among the soldiers in the courtyard, all practical uncles who wanted to kiss him and pet him.

Manrique, at the foot of the homage tower, had been the one squire who'd kept calm during the birth, ordering the others to bring water and linens and keep the fire stoked. Every time Auria saw him, she thought of his wife and child, who were waiting for him on a farm in Segovia. Auria gave continual thanks for his presence, but also spared a thought for his wife's misfortune in being so far from him.

Manrique took the baby from an archer who was holding him awkwardly and cradled him gently until he quieted. He tucked loose swaddling back into place, kissed Jofré's face tenderly, and delivered him into Auria's waiting arms.

"All right, by my count, all fifteen of us have had a turn with the baby. It's time for breakfast, both his and ours."

"Thank you, men, and especially you, Manrique. Good morning," said Auria. Before she entered the homage tower, she opened the slit in her tunic over her breast, and by the time she'd made it to the landing with the arrow hole overlooking the farmland, Jofré's breakfast was almost over.

The crops glinted gold in the morning sunlight, but it was such a small patch, it looked like a single townsperson's garden in the middle of a wide fallow land. Auria gazed up at the few feathery clouds in the sky, which was the color of St. Mary's mantle. Surely the Blessed Mother would answer her prayers soon.

Unnatural movement drew her attention to the river. A knight on horseback, with banners unknown to her, his turban and feathers standing tall, and jewels on the hilt of his sword that sparkled brighter than the sun they reflected, was clearly a Moor. He must've come from the castle over the border. He brought his horse to the river and stopped short. Auria leaned into the arrow slit and studied the terrain around the Moor. Any number of soldiers might be hidden among the trees and rocky outcrops.

Running to the stairs, she clasped Jofré's head to her breast and put her hand over his ear. "Sancho!" she called up the twisting staircase. "Sancho, are you awake? Come quickly!"

Jofré let out a piercing wail in response, so Auria didn't hear her husband come down. He took her by the waist as she looked out the arrow slit, hushing their son.

"What is it, my love?" Sancho whispered in her ear.

Auria backed away from the arrow slit so her husband could look. "See there? A Moorish scout by the river. Will they attack?"

"You don't understand. That's the castellan of Bélmez, the castle we can see across the river on the opposite peak. I could tell by his banners even if I didn't know him already."

"You know him?" Auria asked over Jofré's insistent howls.

"The soldiers from Bélmez looked out for Chincoya for us before we got here. Of course, I went to give the castellan my gratitude, and we still send messages across the river from time to time."

"Why haven't you told me about any of this?"

"You're always busy with Jofré," said Sancho.

Auria put space between her and her husband. "And more."

"What do you mean?"

"I've outfitted the chapel to better honor the Blessed Virgin. I've gotten the household running with almost no help. I've overseen a harvest and a planting, and next year, with the Virgin's help, we'll have enough crops to sustain the hundreds of knights it's going to take to properly defend Chincoya." She paced the chamber, patting her noisy son. But he must've seen the Moor, too, because he would not be comforted.

"That's why it's good to get to know the people in the neighboring castles, in case there's trouble, and you need a friend." Sancho leaned casually against the wall.

"That's the problem! Bélmez is a Moorish castle. If there's trouble, it will come from Bélmez."

"You still don't understand. I know you grew up far from all of this, but there's no cause for alarm. Bélmez belongs to the King of Granada, and he's been paying tribute to Castile. They're practically our vassals, just the way it should've been five hundred years ago, when they were invited to help a traitor and overstayed their welcome. The castellan has written me, inviting me to Bélmez to sign some mutually beneficial pacts in the presence of Christians and Muslims. I knew he was coming today."

"What kind of pacts?"

"I'll swear to protect Bélmez with everything in my power, and they will swear to protect Chincoya."

"No, Sancho. They won't help us. They can't help us."

"He's waiting. I'll go to him."

Auria followed him down into the courtyard, where Jofré's complaints made the soldiers take notice. "We're so close to making this area prosper for the king. I'm only asking you not to throw away all our hard work."

"On the contrary, I'm helping us with this pact. I'll take Manrique with me, and all will be well."

Auria saw Manrique carrying hay to the stables and knew she beheld their hero. "Manrique, come and talk sense to your castellan."

Manrique approached, and Jofré regarded his favorite uncle in reverent silence. The squire smiled and bowed. "What's this, my lord?"

"Come along, and bring two horses. We're going to Bélmez to swear an oath of mutual protection."

"But my lord, we can't cross the river without incurring the king's wrath. Without a royal mandate, crossing the river would be willingly entering enemy territory, and that's treason."

"Thank you, Manrique," said Auria. "Sancho, you know the penalty for treason is death. One way or another, crossing that river will be deadly. Don't leave me a widow. Don't orphan your son!"

"That's enough, Auria and Manrique. The king entrusted this castle to me, and I think it's best to be friendly with Bélmez. Let's go."

Sancho stared ahead at the two soldiers who worked to lower the drawbridge while Auria's tears coated Jofré's wisps of hair. When the bridge was ready, Auria called out, "Manrique." The squire looked back at her, but followed his lord, as Auria knew he must.

Auria ran up the stairs to the battlements, where she could see the river from between the merlons. Her husband and Manrique rode their horses down the twisting path, at a walk that seemed painfully slow from Auria's vantage point.

"If your father truly intends to cross the river," she whispered to Jofré, "I hope that moment never arrives. I would sooner stay in this moment for eternity. It would be so much better if they turned back, and that moment can't come soon enough."

From above, the Christian men looked like children's toys, while the impassive Moor represented some bizarre creature from Apocalypse paintings. What was Sancho walking into?

"Our only hope now is the Blessed Virgin," Auria said. She recited, "Ave Maria, gratia plena," over and over.

The horses stepped down to the level of the river. The Moor waved at the riders, though they were still too far to speak to each other. But while Sancho's horse strode confidently toward the river, Manrique's hesitated. The men gesticulated at each other, reaching to their sides. Then Manrique turned his horse around and started up the incline, back toward Chincoya.

It was only half of what Auria had asked for, but she resolved to show her gratitude to St. Mary.

"Keep the drawbridge down," she shouted to the soldiers at the gate, who were making to crank it back into place, "Manrique is returning!"

Shifting Jofré in her arms, Auria watched as Manrique arrived, and her husband continued without him. The moment his horse set its hoof in the shallow water, a chill ran up her spine. It was not a step anyone could undo.

Sancho brought his horse right up alongside the Moor's, and the men embraced like blood relatives. They turned and disappeared behind the trees and rocks Auria had been so worried about. "St. Mary, save us!"

Manrique appeared at her side and gazed at the river. "I'm sorry, my lady. Neither of us had a sword or any weapon at all. But my lord wouldn't listen, no matter what I said. I couldn't convince him that we needed them. He insisted on going on ahead, and I disobeyed him and came back."

"They've gone to Bélmez together. I don't know what to do," said Auria.

There was no answer Manrique could give. Jofré fussed and Manrique took him and patted him on the back until he quieted. Together, they listened to the drawbridge going up.

"What if Sancho needs to come back?" asked Auria.

"We can't risk the Moor following him inside."

The unnatural silence in the castle was like the moments following the tolling of the bells for a funeral mass at Auria's parish in Segovia. It unfolded throughout the barracks, climbed up the stone walls like ivy, and rose through Auria's feet until it choked her and she collapsed near Manrique's feet. She closed her eyes and imagined Sancho returning to Chincoya safe and sound, into her arms. She wouldn't have to return to Segovia a widow with her head hung low, and no one would ever have to know he'd committed treason crossing the river.

She knew not how many minutes or hours later, Manrique extended his hand to her. "Doña Auria, look!"

She took his hand and pulled herself up to look over the battlement again. Sancho was coming back! But it was nothing like she'd imagined. He was on foot. The castellan of Bélmez rode his horse beside Sancho, and Auria wondered what had happened to Sancho's horse as her husband stumbled through the swift water, soaking his boots. And they kept coming, advancing against Chincoya at the head of what must've been one hundred Moorish soldiers, complete with ladders and trumpeters with garish banners. Was Sancho leading an attack on his own castle?

"St. Mary, save us!" cried Auria, taking Jofré back. "Manrique, get the archers in place."

By the time the squire had returned to the battlement with

the four archers and sent them to man their stations at evenly spaced points, the entire Moorish army was on the Chincoya side of the river and still advancing. When Sancho arrived at the castle slope, a Moorish soldier shoved him and he stumbled forward, barely maintaining his balance. It was then that Auria saw his hands were bound.

"He's a hostage," she said.

Manrique nodded and waved to the archers. They nocked their bows, although the army was too far for an arrow to reach.

Sancho's shouting scaled the castle wall, weak with the effort, and Auria strained to hear.

"King Ibn al Ahmar of Granada knows how many soldiers defend Chincoya. You can see how many soldiers he has. Hand the castle over to them or they'll cut off my head!"

Auria leaned against the battlement, afraid she would faint and drop Jofré. She forgot to breathe.

"Doña Auria, what should we answer?" asked Manrique.

She could see the tension in the squire's face even through her tears. The life of the father of her child forfeit, so many enemy warriors, and so few on their side. But they both knew what had to be done.

She inhaled deeply. "We can't give up Chincoya. We must defend what my husband wouldn't. But please, you respond. I don't think I have the strength."

"Tell the pagan king we will never surrender Chincoya." Manrique's voice crashed against the rocks below. "This castle is King Alfonso's until every one of us is dead."

The army must've heard, because they moved up the hill, toward the ramparts, with ladders, archers, and axes.

Auria lost sight of Sancho in the melee. At least she hadn't seen him killed.

"I'm taking Jofré to safety," she said, and labored down the battlement stairs, unable to feel her legs.

The ten soldiers who weren't archers stood at attention in the courtyard. "You two stay at the gate in case they have the gall to attack there. The rest of you, to the battlements, and bring all the stones, chamber pots, and refuse you can find." Auria wondered if her hoarseness betrayed her fear.

Standing at the foot of the homage tower, she realized there was a much safer place to take her baby. Weaving through the soldiers as they scrambled to find the defensive items she'd named, she found her way to the chapel.

In the dimness, the only light seemed to come from the Virgin's serene expression. Auria heard shouting from the battlements that made her wonder how the Queen of Heaven could remain tranquil. She set Jofré in a basket on the floor, supporting his head on folded linens she must've intended for altar cloths at some calmer time.

"Mother of God, defend this castle and us, your servants," she prayed, trying to look into the Virgin's blue eyes. "And protect your chapel so the infidel Moors won't capture it, find my son, and burn your image."

She didn't know if it was an answer to her prayer, but Auria suddenly knew that she who carried the Infinite inside her need not wait passively for the enemy to come to her. What were one hundred Moors against St. Mary and sixteen of her followers?

She put her hands on either side of the bottom of Mary's carved throne. The image was as light as it had been when Auria carried it at her side from Segovia. "Santiago, watch over my Jofré," she said, nodding at the other saint's figure as she hurried out of the chapel, cradling St. Mary even as she held her Child.

The courtyard was empty of everything but sound. The guards

at the gate cowered under the protection of the wall, but when they saw what Auria was doing, they followed her up the stairs to the battlement. Her archers above were ducking behind merlons to nock their bows, revealing themselves only to shoot straight downward. When she arrived at the top of the stairs, she noted that the other soldiers had already run out of their improvised ammunition. They could only push the tops of the ladders away, protecting themselves with swords, daggers, and shields.

An arrow flew over Auria's head and she instinctively drew the image closer so her cloak covered it.

"What are you doing, Doña Auria?" shouted Manrique.

Auria straightened and held the Virgin and Child out to the squire. "The Moorish army must see who we have on our side."

Manrique gasped and crossed himself, then gingerly grasped the image by the arms.

Auria nodded at an archer, who made way for Manrique. The squire placed the Blessed Mother squarely on the edge of the battlement, where she would be visible all the way in the Kingdom of Granada. From behind, Auria thought her hand looked less like a blessing than a gesture of military or royal domination.

"Let's see what she does." Manrique pulled all fourteen soldiers back from their posts.

A hush fell over the castle again, but it must only have been in Auria's mind, because the ladder landing between the merlons must've made a terrific clatter, and the first Moorish soldier who set foot on the battlement worked his mouth feverishly as he gestured to his fellows, so he must've been shouting.

Auria was terrified by his turban and the flash of his curved sword as he brandished it at the soldiers. But his eyes weren't those of a demon. They looked just like Sancho's or Manrique's.

Auria startled to think he was simply following his commander's orders, and perhaps didn't even agree with them.

A second Moor came over the wall, younger and smaller, someone's son. He fell in with two other Christians while Manrique grappled with the first attacker. The enemies wrestled on foot without weapons until Manrique forced his opponent into a crenel and an archer helped him shove the man so that his body cracked upon the rocks below. Auria wondered if he had a wife and children, and whether they waited for him at Bélmez, or would receive his body with the terrible news several days or weeks from then.

The Moorish trumpets blasted through the apparent silence.

From behind St. Mary, Auria witnessed the ranks fall back. "They're leaving. The Virgin has saved us!"

She turned to see two of her soldiers knock the young Moor down to join the first. A third, blond and panicked, had arrived at the top of the ladder when Manrique pushed into him with his shield, sending both man and ladder far below. All of Chincoya waited, holding their breath, but no more ladders landed, and no one else appeared atop the battlement.

Exhaling prayers of thanks, Auria peered around the image of St. Mary to see the army moving across the river to Bélmez, none looking back. But someone had been left behind. A man was picking his way slowly up the slope.

"Open the drawbridge!" shouted Auria. "Sancho's coming back!"

The entire company crowded down the stairs. While the soldiers worked to crank the drawbridge open, Auria carried the image to the chapel, where Jofré was wailing lustily. She placed St. Mary in her honored spot on the altar, then caught her baby in her arms.

"You're not an orphan, my love," she whispered into his blossom-like ear. "Your father is coming home now. We have so much to give thanks for."

She knelt, and holding her son, she prayed her gratitude even when she heard the uproar of the soldiers receiving Sancho and closing the gate behind him. If he'd learned the lesson the Virgin had taught them that day, he would find her.

Soon enough, through her closed eyelids, she sensed the light from the doorway being blocked. Sancho stood before her with his head down and his hands folded. His wrists were rubbed raw from his bindings and tears in his tunic showed where he'd been grabbed and forced to give up the information about their lack of troops and supplies.

"I'm so sorry, my love. I truly believed the castellan of Bélmez was my friend, and that we were going to swear loyalty today, so that ever after he would be our ally."

Auria stood and might have embraced him if Jofré's warmth in her arms hadn't reminded her what her husband had risked.

"You left us. You nearly lost your life and let the enemy take our castle. Until today, I thought we were both doing the work of the Blessed Virgin and the king. How can I trust you've learned your lesson?"

"I've come to beg your forgiveness," said Sancho.

Auria wept for the husband she'd nearly lost. "It's not my forgiveness you need, my foolish darling. Ask it of St. Mary."

The soldiers crowded into the chapel. Manrique led the others in intoning Gaude Virgo, and when Auria looked at Mary's face, her smile told her all she needed to know.

"The Blessed Mother must forgive you," she told Sancho. "Otherwise, she wouldn't have performed the miracle of bringing you home and making the troops turn back with no losses to us."

"When her image appeared over the battlement, and the soldier fell to his doom, the King of Granada said, 'I profit nothing by continuing this attack and would consider myself foolish to go against Mary, who defends her people.' Even the Moors understand the power of the Mother of God. I'm so grateful you knew better than I did." Sancho took his family into his arms.

Feeling her husband safe and whole, the hymn to the Virgin resonating in her ears, Auria knew Chincoya would be safe for many years to come.

Our Lady's Troubadour

Cantiga 194

Kingdom of Aragón, thirteenth century

In León, they always want me to sing about the siege of Zamora and how El Cid avenged King Sancho. In Castile, I can't get through a recital without a request for the scenes of El Cid's exile, and how he wept at leaving Burgos and his wife and daughters behind. When I'm in Aragón, none of that interests them, so I have to start the tale with the hero's exploits in the lands to the south. Those parts are amusing, and I can make up new names for the Moorish warriors and the strange things they say.

I used to sing about El Cid as much as people wanted, as long as they paid. But what I really liked to do was compose new songs about the miracles of Our Lady. I would hear about new marvels she'd worked as I traveled from place to place, and as I lay on a mattress in a lord's great hall or paced the floor of a private chamber in a governor's palace, I made up new rhyme schemes and filled in the wondrous deeds of the Virgin Mary. It wasn't as easy to compose when I had to bunk in barns or even in the rough.

I'd spent the night in the castle at Barcelona, and wandered through the mountains, wondering a little where I might next find shelter and employment. But the Mother of God has always provided for me, so as I meandered on my donkey, I worked on the verses I'd started the night before. It had a lively rhythm, great for travel.

>*"We must always keep in mind*
>*"The deeds of the Virgin*
>*"Since even the hardest stone accepted them."*

A young man dressed in leather stamped with green leaves and a hunting cap appeared around a bend in the mountainside. "You sing with grace and ease," he said. "Do you seek employment?"

"My name is Munio." I doffed my hat. "I've played at most of the courts in Spain and France. Perhaps you've heard of me? And yes, I'm in need of a place to sing my tales tonight."

"Excellent," he said with a nod. "My lord, Don Gutierre Beltrán, would be happy to lodge you and to hear you this evening. I left the hunting party when I heard your canticle, but I can take you to the palace right now."

"I thank you. I don't think my donkey would be very good at tracking a stag," I joked.

He smiled. "I'm Lope. Follow me."

I dismounted and led my donkey by the reins. Lope took the rein on the other side, looking the animal over. "Your packs aren't very big," he mentioned. He sought footing on the climb up a slope to a much wider road.

"No, I don't need many clothes to travel in summer, and in Barcelona they didn't send me off with many provisions because they were sure I would find more work quickly. I trust St. Mary to see to my needs."

In truth, I'd already snacked on the cheese and bread the royal palace had provided, and they'd been exceedingly generous in a different way. In the bottom of the pack on my side, there were so many coins, I hadn't had a chance to count them yet. Even if I couldn't find work, I could pay for a bed wherever I could find one. But there was no need to mention that.

I followed his lead slowly, encouraging my donkey, and for the final push up onto the road, we tugged at the reins together, making short work of a job that could've lasted hours.

"I would ask why you don't get a horse, but if you spend a lot of time in mountains, even the best traveler wouldn't be as surefooted as your friend here," said Lope, scratching the donkey's ears.

"I think she likes you," I said. I felt certain the Virgin had guided me, or my donkey, anyway, to a most profitable evening.

I told Lope about the song I was composing for the Queen of Heaven, and that I knew the seven noble knights of Lara, Fernán González and the rest of the Counts of Castile, Bernardo del Carpio, and the Bell of Huesca, which is popular in other regions of the Kingdom of Aragón, but he said what I expected: "Do you know the song of El Cid?"

"I know it from beginning to end, from Zamora to Burgos to Valencia."

"Good. I'm sure my lord will want to hear it all."

I felt a bit tired after wandering the mountains all day, but I knew that the longer I sang and played, the more opportunities the residents and guests would have to slip coins into my bag, so I couldn't complain at the prospect.

Around a bend in the road, the town appeared, climbing up a hillside with its golden castle on top, bigger than the town itself. I stopped, awestruck.

"That's Don Gutierre's castle?"

"You haven't heard of him?" Lope asked. "King Jaume granted him this castle personally in perpetuity for all his heirs. There's no more powerful lord in the Kingdom of Aragón."

"No, I suppose not," I said.

We wound through the streets of the town, circling slowly up to the castle. Everyone we passed greeted Lope as a friend, and sometimes he told them who I was. "He'll be singing the entire song of El Cid tonight. Join us for the feast!"

"I take requests, too," I added. "And I've just been in Barcelona. I'm sure you'll want to hear all the news."

This was met with assurances that they would attend. I hoped there would be a lot of wine to keep my throat lubricated for what was sizing up to be a long night. By the time we arrived at the castle gate, the voices of all the townspeople were echoing up the mountainside. "Finish your work! A jongleur's in the castle tonight!"

Lope told the watchman who I was, and I made a theatrical bow. It was more than enough to gain admittance, and we accompanied my donkey into an outer bailey abuzz with activity. Some were expected, such as currying horses and carrying baskets of victuals to and fro, and some surprising, such as two men collecting stones and kindling to make three fire pits.

"Has there been news from the hunt?" Lope asked one.

"They sent a messenger ahead. They've taken a stag and two does."

"Don Gutierre must also be the best hunter in all Christendom," I said.

"It's a good thing, too," Lope said. "The entire town is coming to enjoy this venison."

I followed him as he led my donkey to be brushed down as if she were the finest warhorse returned from battle. When I saw that she would be well cared for, I lifted the two-sided pack off her neck by the buckle that held them together.

"Your belongings will be safe here, too, if you want to leave them," said Lope.

"I need my rebec to play and my change of clothes, since I've been traveling," I explained. It was true, but I also hoped he didn't hear the coins clinking on one side.

If he noticed, he didn't say anything, and escorted me to a chamber where he and a few other high-ranking servants slept. "You can stay with us. We'll get an extra bedroll before the night is over. Now I'll let you get settled, tune your instrument."

"Won't I have time for that later? I can help you in the dining hall now."

"Take the opportunity. It's going to be a busy night." He closed the door softly.

I laid my pack on the nearest bedroll and decided to change my clothes. I extracted the coins from Barcelona and wrapped them in my hose, tunic, and even my undershirt, counting as I went. It was far too much cash to travel with. I made up my mind to spend the night in that castle and head directly home to Navarra the next morning. I would stash most of it at my house, but I also had a new idea to get a horse to travel in a little more style. Maybe I would hire an illuminator to make a codex of my compositions for St. Mary.

I stuffed the coins in the clothes back into the empty pack, and they no longer made any noise. Satisfied with my plans, I got dressed in the fresh clothes and took my rebec and bow out of the wrappings. Looking at the sagging strings, I could tell it was severely out of tune.

A knock on the door prompted me to say, "Come in." Two maids laden with sheets and ticking entered, and I greeted them.

"You must be the jongleur," said one.

"And troubadour of Our Lady," I replied nodding.

"That's Mendo's bed. We'll make you a nicer one over here," said the other. They piled the bedding on the floor across the room from me.

"I would help you, but Lope tells me I need to get this rebec in tune."

"Go right ahead, sir. We won't take but a moment."

They set to work. I tightened the pegs to begin with and then tested with the bow. The instrument let out such a screech that the women jumped.

"Sorry!" I said.

They laughed. "You'll have to do better than that for Don Gutierre. He has excellent musical sense."

I exaggerated a grimace, adjusted the pegs again, and drew the bow across one string at a time until all four were markedly improved. I looked up, and the women had finished making a cozy-looking bed and stood waiting to see what I would do. I started a lively dance, and they gamely linked arms and pranced between the bedrolls. That's how Lope found us.

"Come along, Munio," he said. "You'll want to eat something before the banquet gets started."

I carried my pack on my shoulder and my rebec before me, careful not to jostle it. When we arrived in the kitchen, Lope pointed to a place at a table that had been cleared. I set the rebec down gently, afraid even looking at it would knock it out of tune, and sat on the bench before the small plate of food amongst the bustling cooks and kitchen boys.

"The hall is prepared and the lord and lady will arrive soon. You've got a long evening ahead of you. Eat up!" He clapped me on the back and nearly sent a crusty loaf of bread into my instrument. I was too busy making sure it hadn't been touched to ask him whether I would be allowed to partake of the feast.

It turned out that I wasn't. As soon as I had gulped down some bread and a chicken thigh, with nothing to wash it down, I was ushered into the great hall. Long tables, or many placed together, lined all four walls with gaps between them for servants to weave their way through the room. All the tables were covered with bright cloths and all the chairs occupied. Other people who looked like they might eat standing up or seated on the floor milled about in the center. The noise of them, all so excited about the feast, filled my senses, and I might've wandered away, but a maid told me to wait there on the side until I was called.

A hush descended on the hall as the first cook paraded through with an enormous platter heaped with the roasted meat from the hunt. He seemed hardly able to support its weight, and it hit the table in front of the lord and lady with a resonant thud. Both lord and lady picked a bit of meat from the top, and it crumbled in their hands.

"A most satisfactory hunt, my lord," said the lady. "The juice is running down my sleeve!"

Everyone laughed for joy. Don Gutierre gestured to the cook to bring the rest of the dishes. The talking, shouting, and laughing started up again as if it had never stopped, this time accompanied by cooks and kitchen boys running platters out to all the tables. I witnessed countless near collisions between them and the standing diners, but it was clear they were well-practiced.

Don Gutierre's voice resounded from the head table. "I'm told there's a jongleur. Bring him out!"

I'd completely lost track of where Lope had gone, but several kitchen boys pushed through the crowd to allow me to take my place in the center of the tables. I set my sack before me in case anyone felt moved to throw coins into it and got my first good look at my hosts. The lord's and lady's clothes had gold thread that shimmered in the candlelight, and their eyes glimmered expectantly at me.

"Do you know El Cid?" asked Don Gutierre.

"Of course, my lord," I tried to say, but my voice cracked. Then I started coughing. I wasn't sure if my throat was dry from bread or nerves. "I'm sorry. Could I have some wine?"

Don Gutierre pointed at the young servant next to the table near him. He filled a mug from the wineskin and ran it to me. After I'd downed half the mug, I felt good enough to sing of the death of the first King Fernando and the fratricidal war that followed while the diners feasted, chatted, and sometimes sang along. By the time El Cid's eyes were filled with tears leaving Burgos, I had to ask for more refreshment. I sang them through Valencia, and when I asked again for more wine, a more experienced-looking servant finally caught on and brought a whole wineskin.

By then, the food had been devoured, and a few people approached and laid coins at the tip of my pack, just as I'd hoped. I lifted the corner to make the coins disappear inside every time I could find an excuse to free my hands.

And so, I was able to continue through the affront at Corpes and the hero's honorable death, and into the latest news about the Morisco uprising in Murcia and the Aragonese King Jaume's response, taking swigs as necessary and hiding coins deeper into the pack as more people contributed.

I played my latest composition for Our Lady, and it seemed to please most, but then Don Gutierre requested I play a dance. Perhaps he needed to wake the guests up a little so they wouldn't all sleep in his castle. I'm pretty sure most of them did, anyway. I sawed away at my poor rebec and the crowd's tunics churned around me in a confusion of colors until one of my strings broke.

I reached into my pack to see if I could string another one, but found only coins. I looked up to make sure no one had noticed just how much had gone into the pack. Then I checked the wineskin, and it was empty, too. The guests were already making up for the lack of music, clapping their hands, shouting, and singing as best they could, so I stood up straight and announced, "My broken string tells me the evening has come to an end for me. I thank my lord and lady and all of the guests at these revels."

A few people waved at me, bidding me good night. I hefted my pack onto my shoulder and made my way back to the servants' bower. It had been a good night.

I woke with a headache, and I couldn't tell if it came from the wine or from using my pack, full of hard, cold coins, as a pillow. Quite a bit of light was filtering through the shutters, and I was still resolved to go home and unload all the cash, so I thought I'd best be on my way. I eased out of the comfortable bedding, containing groans because the other beds were full of sleeping forms, including that of Lope next to me.

The rebec lay on the floor beside my sack. I wasn't sure how to pack it without crushing it among so many coins, so I left the room the way I had entered, with the pack on my shoulder and the rebec in my hand.

In the hallway, two men from the town I remembered from the feast lay snoring their cares away. I passed the great hall, and saw quite a few others in similar positions, and even a man and woman in a loving embrace. I crossed myself and said, "Ave Maria," then thought perhaps I would call on Juana in my town and see if she wanted to marry me. She probably wouldn't like to travel as much as I do.

The empty pit in my stomach led me to the kitchen, where a few cooks were stoking the fires. One asked me if I would like some porridge.

"No, thank you. I start my journey home right away. Do you have some bread, perhaps?"

"There's nothing left after the feast," said the cook.

"Here's some honey pastry," said a kitchen boy.

I thanked him profusely and finished it before I came to the well in the outer bailey. The pastry started soaking up some of the previous night's wine even as I drank from the well and washed up. I observed the remnants of the fire pits from the venison I'd never gotten to sample, then rearranged a few things in my pack, letting the coins fall to the bottom, and wrapped my rebec in its cloth. I was easing it into the barely adequate free space when someone walked up behind me and spoke, jarring me. Another of the strings broke with a sad twang, even inside the wrapping.

"Headed out already?" It was Lope. "This is Mendo. You'll have seen him last night. We'll help you get your donkey down the slope and on the main road."

How long had they been watching me? Had they seen some of the coins in my bag? I did recognize Mendo from when he brought me the wineskin. I couldn't think of a good reason not to let them come with me, and even felt a bit wicked for doubting their motives. It was a courteous offer I should answer in kind.

"That sounds like a fine idea," I said. They helped me find my donkey among the horses. I loaded the pack across her neck and gave her a few encouraging pats.

As we traveled, all on foot, Lope and Mendo laughed and joked about the feast the night before, though I felt too drowsy to join in. In my distraction, I couldn't help but hum my latest tune for St. Mary.

"Hey, you sang very well last night," said Mendo. "I don't think anyone's ever sung the entire Cid, much less kept going after that."

"Thank you. I don't mind working hard," I rasped. I felt my voice ready to abandon me again.

"You must gather a lot of coin," Mendo continued. "I watched almost everyone put something in your sack, one by one."

I couldn't think what to respond, and my throat protested with a cough. "Did either of you bring a wineskin?"

"No," said Lope. "But if you go south on the smaller road, there's a town with a couple of taverns. We're almost at the junction."

"I don't think I want to go south," I whispered. "I'm trying to get home to Navarra now."

"South is probably the fastest way out of these mountains," said Mendo. "Then circling around them to go north on the plain will be faster."

We'd come to the place where the roads nearly met, so I let go of my donkey's reins to prepare for the steep trip down.

"But that doesn't matter," said Lope. "You're not going to Navarra."

He pushed me squarely in the chest with the flat of both hands. I fell down the slope head first.

Before I knew what was happening, my helpless motion stopped. My legs had become tangled in brambles and broken my fall. All I could manage was a strangled cry.

I tried looking up the slope, but the angles were wrong, so I couldn't see what was happening. But Mendo's voice echoed off the hillsides. "Did you hear that? He's still alive."

I worked at the brambles to see if I could run away, but thorns sliced at my fingers. Lope and Mendo peeked over the ridge and saw me below, helpless.

"Have you got a sharp knife?" Lope asked Mendo. "Give it to me. I'm going down there to kill him."

"No! Take my donkey. I have nothing else in the world," I said, but if they heard anything, it probably sounded like whimpering.

"It's my knife," said Mendo. "I should probably kill him."

"I won't accuse you of anything, only leave me alone!" I tried, coughing.

"I found him in the mountains when you were with the hunting party," said Lope, "so he's my responsibility. Where are some sticks? We can cast lots to find out who should do it."

They were monsters. I realized there was no talking to them, even if they could hear me. I reached desperately for the brambles around my legs, feeling my doom upon me. I was all by myself, with no friend to protect me.

But I always had a protector, whether I thought I was alone or not. That was when my voice returned to me. I shouted such that they could probably hear back in Don Gutierre's castle. "Mother of the Merciful King, save me! Don't let them kill me! Defend me without delay!"

When my voice finished echoing off the hillside, I kept perfectly still, listening. Lope and Mendo said nothing, made no noise. Had they gone? I couldn't be sure. In my stillness, I found that I was able to reach my eating knife in my belt, and I sawed the brambly prison away from my legs. I hesitated to move because there had still been no noise from above and no way to know what was happening. Suddenly, a great braying resounded, and I felt drawn to check on my donkey.

My legs hadn't suffered more than a few scrapes, so I climbed the slope and crouched at the edge to observe without being seen.

My donkey was where I'd left her, stamping her feet in agitation. But what surprised me was that in spite of the silence, Lope and Mendo were there, too. They stood perfectly still with their arms outstretched, as if they had frozen in the instant when Lope tried to take the knife from Mendo. I waited a moment, and as it seemed they never changed their position in the slightest, not even to breathe, I stood up to their level and approached them. I circled them and looked into their eyes, which were the only things about them that moved. So they hadn't somehow died standing there.

I worked the knife out of Mendo's clenched hand and threw it down the slope, just in case. I tapped his shoulder with a single finger, and he fell over like a tree. His face was so contorted with pain he couldn't express that I almost felt sorry for him.

"Why would the servant of such a rich lord want to steal the lowly possessions of a traveling jongleur?" I asked. He blinked and his eyes rolled about, but his mouth never moved.

I left Lope standing alone and turned to my donkey. "Did you see what happened?" I caressed her behind the ears to calm her down. "I think this is a miracle. They say that the mere invocation of the Blessed Virgin is as terrible as a mighty army to evildoers. I think this is the Glorious Queen's answer to my plea. We have quite the new song to compose for the folks back home."

I checked that the pack was secure and considered how I

was going to get my donkey down the slope. "I really could've used your help," I told Lope and Mendo. "What a shame you weren't listening when I sang my song for St. Mary. It would've convinced you to leave your evil ways."

I decided to take the higher road. It would probably be faster to leave the mountains, anyway. I led my donkey past the servants' deathly quiet bodies.

"Don't worry," I told them. "The Mother of God wouldn't leave you to die. I'm sure when I'm safe, you'll be able to move again."

It wasn't for me to say. I couldn't know what other villainous deeds those two might've done, and perhaps the Ultimate Judge would decide to condemn them while they couldn't explain their sins away. But I didn't feel right leaving them in that state.

When I came to a bend in the road, I looked back, and Lope appeared to lower his arm as slowly as the movement of a sundial's shadow. I knew better than to wait for them to catch up to me.

Since then, I travel all over, singing my miracle in praise of the Virgin, who always saves those who call on her. When they ask for El Cid, I sing my miracle first, and the deeds of that great warrior don't seem as marvelous anymore. Everyone calls the miracle the Glorious Queen worked for me the noblest and most beautiful story of all.

Tournament of Honor

Cantiga 195

Languedoc, southern France, thirteenth century

At my childhood home, my mother had an herb garden that used to blossom beautifully in the springtime. My father stopped getting out of bed when he had too much sorrow for my mother's passing. I was heartbroken, too, but I suspected that neither my mother nor the Glorious Virgin wanted us both to lie down and waste away. I thought it would honor my mother's life if I tended to her garden.

I only wanted to check whether the plants needed water, but the recent rains had had the opposite effect. Weeds had crept in between the carefully selected and tended shrubs. So I hitched up my skirts, knelt in the soil, and started pulling up the invaders. Some of the roots were deep, making for hard work, and the sun was hot. But I hardly noticed the time passing while I remembered helping my mother in that very place and sang a song I knew in praise of St. Mary.

"Rose of all roses, flower of all flowers, lady of all ladies…"

I looked up and stopped my singing because there was a stranger in our garden. I gathered that he was a knight because he rode a warhorse covered in eagle heraldry, he wore his body armor, and a sword, shield, and helmet hung conspicuously from the saddle. I hadn't seen anyone like that come to our house before, so I wasn't sure what to say or expect.

He looked at me for a few moments before he spoke.

"How old are you?"

"Sixteen." I had nothing to hide, I thought.

A closed-mouth smile crossed his face, and his eyes glinted but remained lifeless. "Is your father home?"

It wouldn't have occurred to me to lie. "Yes, he's just inside."

The knight dismounted.

"Wait. What are you doing?" I asked, to no answer. I followed the knight to our front door, where he knocked forcefully with his strengthened leather glove. When no one answered, he knocked harder.

My father opened the door, his linen nightshirt deeply creased and his knees sticking out for anyone to see. He saw the visitor and ran his hand through his hair, leaving it standing up even more crazily than before. I wasn't sure whether to feel embarrassed or frightened.

"What brings you here, Sir Knight?" my father said, his voice still broken with sleep.

"My name is Don Ordoño de Alquézar, and I was passing through here with my regiment on our way to the tournament in Toulouse. I heard your daughter singing and came to see who she was." He spoke quickly, as if he hardly had time for the few words he said. The only pause was to look my father up and down like a horse he was considering for purchase. "You seem as if you could use some money. How much would you take for your daughter?"

My father snapped out of his stupor, and I inserted myself between the men.

"No!" I shrieked at the knight. "What do you mean?"

"Do you want to marry my daughter?" asked my father, tilting his head and squinting.

"Not exactly," said the knight. "But I will provide for her. She'll never want for anything."

I took my father's hands and knelt. "You know I've only ever wanted to become a nun and worship St. Mary. You won't let this stranger take me away, and dishonorably, not even considering marriage, will you?"

He wrested out of my grip and patted me on the head, but addressed the knight. "How much are you offering?"

"I have a hundred *maravedíes* in my saddle I could give you right now."

I had never seen my father's eyes so wide. "So much?"

"It's not a problem. I'm going to gain it back, and more, when I win the tournament."

I stood and tried to look my father in the eye. "That's what you're worried about?" I couldn't fathom what was going on. "That's the value of my life?"

"A hundred *maravedíes* would take away so many worries for me, daughter." He tried to kiss my cheek, but I dodged him. "And you know, now that your mother's gone, I could never provide you the dowry you deserve without help. Look at him. Is he so bad?"

I couldn't see Don Ordoño at all beyond what he was trying to do—buy me. To use for purposes I could only guess at. I was speechless.

"The longer this takes, the harder we'll have to ride to catch up with my regiment," said the knight.

My father spoke the last words I would ever hear him say. "Bring me the coins."

"St. Mary, save me," I managed before I passed out.

When I opened my eyes, I saw horses and armed riders all around me. My back ached horribly because I'd been slumped against Don Ordoño's horse's neck for what must've been some time. I couldn't sense anything tying me down, and wondered if I could slip off the horse while it was moving. But I also doubted I was strong enough to straighten up on my own and avoid being trampled by the rest of the regiment. A tremendous sneeze made the decision for me, forcing me upright against a large body in armor that could only be Don Ordoño. He put an arm around my waist to hold me there.

"So, you've come back to me. I'm glad. We're going to have a delightful night together."

That morning, I'd thought I was going to revive my mother's garden so my father and I could sell some plants, and eat some, and not starve. My father's solution was certainly quicker. What he'd done for the sake of money fell on me like a downpour. I buried my face in my hand.

"All these years I've kept intact, only to be sold like a broodmare." I could hardly breathe through the sobbing.

"Hush, little one. There's no reason to cry. I'll treat you well." Don Ordoño tightened his grip around my waist and put his cheek next to mine. Perhaps he was trying to console me, or perhaps merely keep my agitation from disturbing the horse, which had already changed its stride. "What's your name?"

"María," I wailed. "I was named for the Mother of God, but

I'm too unfortunate to be compared to her. A fate worse than what I've most dreaded has come true."

Don Ordoño straightened up and loosened his grip around me. I couldn't tell why. I twisted and looked up, trying to see his face, but my vision was too blurry.

"And today is Saturday, St. Mary's day. I've always kept vigil in honor of the Virgin Mother in order to earn the blessed life my own mother told me about, which I've never doubted and always believed in. Today that vigil is to be broken in the worst way."

Don Ordoño pulled gently on the reins, and his horse slowed. Other knights passed ahead. Some made comments like, "Hey, champion! What are you doing?"

"What *are* you doing?" I asked.

He whispered in my ear as if he wanted none of the other knights to hear. "I understand you're a religious girl. I should observe St. Mary's day, too, if I want her protection in the tournament, and because I owe it to her after the many times she's helped me in battle."

I still didn't know what he was doing, but curiosity stopped my weeping. It seemed my doom was delayed until at least the next day. I dried my face on my sleeves.

Gripping my thigh, Don Ordoño said, "Flaín," which turned out to be the name of his squire, who rode alongside us. Both horses came to a complete stop, and finally the regiment passed ahead.

"I'm taking this whiny girl to the Abbey of St. Clement in Toulouse. I'll rejoin the regiment outside the city at the tournament afterward," said Don Ordoño. "I shouldn't be long, but let the captain know if he asks about me before I'm back."

The squire nodded. "As you say, my lord." He dared to wink

at me, but I couldn't respond in my bewilderment. Was he accustomed to covering for his knight while he stole maidens away from their families? The squire spurred his horse to catch up to the regiment, and I was alone with Don Ordoño.

"What are we doing at the convent?" I shrilled. "Do you know the nuns there?"

He didn't answer, but adjusted his hold on me so that I hardly noticed it anymore. We continued on our way, leaving me to wonder if I was going to end up losing everything in an abbey. Perhaps he had an agreement with fallen nuns there, and a large bed and my complete ruin awaited. It wasn't the trip to a convent I'd always hoped for. The horse protested loudly as I pulled at his mane nervously.

"Hey, rip out your own hair, but leave my horse alone," was all Don Ordoño said.

The sun beat down on us in its last brilliance before evening as we entered the gates of Toulouse and followed the sentry's directions to the abbey. The townspeople hardly glanced at us, and I wondered if many knights brought young ladies through the town, whether to the abbey or elsewhere.

We found the enormous white stone building by its bell tower, and rode right up to its curtain wall. Don Ordoño dismounted and helped me down, then kept my hand in his powerful grip, curbing my instinct to run away.

He rapped at the door the same way he had at my house. I tried flexing my knuckles while we waited to distract myself from the terror, but I couldn't move my hand at all.

The door squeaked open a sliver, and a short nun in black squinted at us.

"My name is Don Ordoño de Alquézar, and I have a novice for you. You can tell the abbess that she's very orderly, and if you need a dowry, I'm going to the tournament, and I will donate my winnings."

My mouth dropped open. The nun screwed up her face even further, grunted, and shut the door again.

"You've brought me to become a nun?" It was what I'd always wanted but never thought possible. It wasn't the horror of violation and infamy I'd expected. I could hardly believe the day was ending in a way so different from how it began.

"This is what you want, isn't it?" asked the knight.

"It's more than I would have dared pray for." I held Don Ordoño's hand in both of mine. "That's the second time today you're paying for my life."

"The first purchase was villainous. The second, well, I hope it will make up for the first." He nodded curtly. It seemed he wanted forgiveness, but all I had to offer was wonder.

The nun opened the door, this time wide enough for us to pass through. My eyes could hardly take in everything as she led us along a kind of courtyard, then a passageway illuminated by torches along the wall, then the halls of a cloister with too many archways to count, framed by fantastic carved figures and saints. The nun stopped in front of a door off the cloister and tapped it ajar.

"The abbess is expecting you," she said.

Don Ordoño nodded at the nun, and she scurried away. He opened the door wide, presenting what looked to me like the most magnificent study in the world. A row of five books took up the shelf on the back wall, and we made our way between various tables with coffers or reliquaries.

The abbess, dressed in an undyed tawny tunic as if to brag of her humility, eyed us from behind a lectern with an inkwell and pages upon it, quill poised in the middle of a word. Near the window, a nun in black looked up at us for a moment, then continued copying a manuscript with gold initials and much scribbling in the margins.

Don Ordoño bowed, and I did something like a curtsy, never parting my gaze from the abbess's judgment.

The abbess set down her quill. "I'm told this girl wants to become a novice. Who is she?"

"Her name is María, and there is no one who wants to serve St. Mary more. She's very devout, too devout, in fact, for the marriage plans I had for her," said Don Ordoño.

"And you are?"

"Don Ordoño de Alquézar, her guardian. I've never known her to be disobedient, and she always keeps St. Mary's vigil on Saturdays."

"Except today," the abbess grunted.

"Abbess, I've brought María today because I'm participating in the tournament just outside the city starting on Monday. I'm sure to win all the prizes, and I pledge my winnings as her dowry. In that regard, you won't find even a countess who can bring greater benefit to this abbey."

"Is that so?" said the abbess. She stepped out from behind the lectern to face the knight more closely. "If you're expecting us to take her right now, I'm afraid you'll have to give us something right now."

Don Ordoño looked at me, but I shook my head. I was already poor, without having taken any vow.

"Would a guarantee do?" he asked the abbess. "You know a knight's vow is his duty, and I'd be willing to leave a written record."

"I'm afraid not. We can't operate on promises." The abbess glowered at the knight's hands, which were full of jeweled rings.

The other nun watched us raptly from the window. I gazed into the faces in the room, trying to determine if my fate was to spend the night in the military camp, after all, for want of a few coins.

Don Ordoño sighed. He turned to me and pulled a ring with a sapphire bigger than his pupil off his left hand. He placed it delicately in my palm. "This ring with the blue color of the Mother of God has brought me much fortune for many years. May it now bring good fortune to you."

Tears filled my eyes. I could hardly believe his sacrifice. I knelt before the abbess and clasped her hands around the ring. "Abbess, please accept me as a novice."

"She won't disappoint you," Don Ordoño said behind me. "And the tournament is this week. You'll have a dowry beyond your fondest wishes by next Saturday."

The abbess slipped the ring onto her thumb, which was lightly twisted like the rest of her fingers. Looking at the ring and not at me, she put her hand on my head, and I felt the heat of the long day under the sun in my part.

"I accept you, daughter María, as a novice at our abbey, pending receipt of the dowry promised by your guardian."

I stood and kissed her hands, and Don Ordoño did the same. I jumped at the sudden clang of the church bell.

"It's time for Vespers liturgy," said the abbess.

"Of course," I said, recovering.

"Sor Catalina," said the abbess, and the nun at the lectern set down the quill she'd been holding idly. "Please escort our new novice to the church for Vespers. Don Ordoño, I assume you can find your own way out. I'll join you ladies in the chapel shortly."

The three of us made obeisance and entered the cloister hall, looking questions at each other while the bells finished ringing.

The nun had a sweet, rounded face, and I decided to take the chance that she would be more understanding than the abbess.

"Please, Sor Catalina, take us to the front door and let me say goodbye to my guardian."

She glanced at the church door. First one nun, then groups of two and three, appeared from different passageways and entered the church, casting sidelong glances at us.

Sor Catalina grasped my hand. "All right, but we should hurry."

We hurried through the passageway and courtyard, and too soon, because I hadn't had time to think of what to say, we arrived at the front door. Sor Catalina lifted the bar, and the knight and I faced each other, one on each side of the doorway. Don Ordoño's horse awaited him outside, nipping at the weeds along the edge of the wall.

I took his hand in mine. "Thank you," I breathed.

"Don't," he said, withdrawing his hand. "I deserve no thanks. Only pray for me. Make sure I end up in the same place you do, so both of us can meet the Queen of Heaven."

"I will. Never doubt it."

He smiled wistfully and raised his hand, which glittered a bit less without the sacrificed ring. I didn't let Sor Catalina close the door until he mounted and rode away down the street.

I might've stood there speechless for some time, reliving everything that had happened to me that day, but Sor Catalina grabbed my hand again and practically ran with me.

"Are you sure you know what you're getting into?" she asked in the passageway. "Abbess Blanche has a reputation for meanness. Surely there's some other abbey close to where you live."

I stopped short before a column capital with the Holy Mother and her Child. "I believe St. Mary brought me here. This is the only way I could ever have become a nun like I've always wanted. I have only thanks in my heart."

I stayed at the back of the nave during Vespers prayers and copied everything the nuns were doing. Then Sor Catalina showed me to a cell occupied by another novice. Teresa was the daughter of a duke and three years younger than me. Nonetheless, I was glad to have her there, because she had already been at the abbey for a year, so she could soothe any doubt that came to my mind.

Teresa lent me a blue novice's habit until I could put together one or two of my own and secured my hair modestly under the coif. It felt tense, and as we ate brown bread and vegetable soup in the refectory, I kept moving my head, seeking some kind of comfort. I looked at the long table, the nuns there to praise St. Mary like I was, the rafters holding up the roof, and the nun who read in Latin from a balcony in the wall. I wondered when she would eat, but mainly longed for the day when I could cut my hair off and be done with it.

A nun from the head table tapped my shoulder and said the abbess was asking for me. I laid my spoon in the soup bowl and crossed the refectory, feeling everyone's gaze on me. I bowed my head before Abbess Blanche.

"Rest well tonight, María." Her gaze flitted to my awkward headdress and habit and then to my hands. "You're going to have to earn your keep until your guardian gives us your dowry." I nodded, unsure whether to return to my spot on the bench. "But that doesn't mean you're excused from any prayers. I recommend you go to sleep right after Compline. I'll send someone to tell you what you have to do before Matins."

Before Matins. I knew that office would take place several hours before dawn. With so many thoughts flooding my spirit,

I wondered how I would wedge in the rest I needed. Indeed, I was barely able to follow what the other nuns were doing during Compline, even with Teresa's help.

Back in our cell, Teresa tried to fluff my bolster, but it remained like a rock at the head of my bed. I lay cradled in the cot in complete darkness, wondering what tasks the abbess would set to me, what my father was doing with his stacks of coins, and most of all about Don Ordoño, why he'd had such a miraculous change of heart, and whether he really would return to pay my dowry for the abbey.

I tried to imagine him winning the tournament. His physical strength and confidence predicted that outcome, but his ring on the abbess's thumb wouldn't leave my mind's eye alone.

My eyes didn't stay shut for longer than a moment that night. I felt like it had to have dawned several times over, but a nun came into the room with her beeswax candle to wake me, and when we were in the middle of the cloister, I looked up at a black sky, without moonlight.

The nun instructed me to bring five buckets full of water from the well to the kitchen for the cooks to make breakfast, then go to the church for Matins. She left me to it, surely to attend to whatever her duties were at that time of night. The cypress tree, whispering in the slightest breeze and pointing toward God, was my only company as I figured out how to heft the full bucket and carry a candle by myself so I had some hope of finding my way through the passages.

There was no one in the kitchen but a cat, so I decided to dump the water into the enormous cauldron they would probably use to make porridge. The muscles in my legs as well as my arms ached when I did this for the fifth time, and the bells rang out calling the congregation to Matins. Teresa stood with me and handed me her prayer book, saying she had the responses memorized.

My arm protested the weight of the small, decorated volume. "That's very kind," I whispered, "but I can't read, anyway."

"Oh." She took the book back and turned to the correct page, pointing to the lines of figures representing what we were chanting, but I could hardly see the illustrations in the light from the torches on the wall.

At the end of the prayers, Teresa took me out back into the abbey grounds, where we doled out disgusting meals to the hogs, who ate greedily in the early light with an energy I envied. Teresa chatted pleasantly with me in spite of the hour and my inability to hold up my end. It was already time for Lauds when we finished. After that liturgy, the nun who'd opened the door to Don Ordoño and me what seemed like years before gave me rough cloth and a bar of soap and told me to fill a bucket and scrub the church floor.

I couldn't help but sigh, working up the energy to go back to the well.

"The abbess said you didn't look like a hard worker," said the nun, gazing at me over her nose.

Where would she have gotten that idea? "She's wrong," I said, and hurried into the cloister for the water.

My scrubbing of the church floor was complicated by the continual comings and goings of the nuns who set up different furniture, candles, plates, and chalices for the next office. Some of them tried to step around the wet stones I'd already cleaned, but some tracked dirt as if they'd been in the fields ploughing. Every time I wiped my brow, I knocked my coif out of place and had to stop to line it up again through guesswork. I was standing in the apse, cloth in hand, thinking I'd have to completely redo my work, when the bells tolled again for Prime. My head was already spinning with exhaustion, and the loud sound made my knees buckle.

I was rescrubbing around the choir seat closest to the transept when the abbess strode into the apse from the nave.

"María." Her voice echoed down to me, full of judgment. "Is this all you've done?"

I stood and straightened my veil. "I couldn't help it, Abbess. There was only me to do all this floor in a few minutes, and everyone was walking through."

"Your guardian was wrong about you. You're the worst novice we've ever had." She slapped my wrist, and her rings bruised me, though I noticed her thumb was naked. "Go and stand with Sor Berenguela. Perhaps she can set you straight."

She settled into her chair behind the altar, and I took my bucket and cloths to the sacristy before scurrying to the back of the congregation to find Teresa.

"Which one is Sor Berenguela?" I asked her.

Teresa pointed to a tall nun in black in the middle of the nave. She seemed to sense we were talking about her, because she looked back at us. I shrank under her severe stare, but knew I couldn't disobey the abbess and make her think even worse things about Don Ordoño. I wove among the crowd until I was by her side.

"Sor Berenguela? Abbess Blanche says I'm to stay with you now," I said, facing the altar.

"Are you the terrible new novice?"

"My name is María," I muttered. Her question didn't invite further confidences, and I spent the prayers trying not to draw attention to myself. At the end, Sor Berenguela didn't look to make sure I followed her, but I did my best, and mercifully, we ended up in the refectory to break our fast.

I gulped at the porridge in the hope that it would restore something of my devotion to St. Mary or at least wake me up a little. Instead, the tasteless lumps seemed to slow me down further. My eyelids lowered against my will. When I snapped them open again, I felt Sor Berenguela's steady gaze on me. But somehow, she didn't seem as judgmental as the abbess. Perhaps she was merely curious about me.

"Sor Berenguela, what labor will we attend to between now and Terce?" I asked in the most genteel way I could think of. It seemed unlikely this nun, with the subtle lines around her eyes, creased mouth, and noble airs, would spend the rest of the morning scrubbing floors with me.

"I'm to oversee you doing the hardest work in the garden."

"The garden?" My spoon clattered to the table. "My mother had a garden. I loved working with her there. The smell of the earth, the buzzing insects. Growing things. What kind of things do you grow?"

"The abbey has vegetables, herbs, and medicinal plants for our use and for when the townspeople need our help."

I clasped my hands to my heart. "I can hardly wait to see it."

Another nun across the table from me shushed me. I hadn't thought I'd raised my voice. It didn't seem to matter, because Sor Berenguela was smiling at me. It wasn't an expression I expected to come easily to her.

She glanced up at the balcony where the nun read in Latin. I hadn't noticed the droning voice this time, and much less that the reading had stopped. "Are you finished?" said Sor Berenguela. "Shall we go now?"

I stood up from the bench and held out my hand, and she gently guided me past where Teresa and I had slopped the hogs to a large enclosure lush with green leaves in every shape and size. It was hard to believe so much land was on the other side of the stone wall I'd crossed through the day before from muddy city streets full of carts and horses.

Sor Berenguela gestured to the fields beyond. "We have wheat and rye the abbess will probably make you work with sometime, but for now, we'll stay right here."

The veil started to make sense as it shielded me from the sun that rose and strengthened its heat throughout our hours kneeling in the garden. Sor Berenguela demonstrated the differences between the herbs and plucked a few for the cooks to use at the midday meal. I surprised her by knowing that borage, with its pretty blue flowers, could help to cool the humors.

"My mother taught me that once when my papa had a fever."

"Were you with your parents long? Abbess Blanche told me you arrived with a guardian."

"I remember my mother well," I sputtered. "I went with Don Ordoño when she died."

"I'm sorry to hear that," said Sor Berenguela, patting my hand. We were both filthy with dirt by that time. "It's not easy growing up without a mother."

"No," I said, and though I was already grown up, my mother had only gone to Heaven months before, and I started to cry.

Sor Berenguela helped me stand and took me into her arms. "You've had the very good fortune of coming to this abbey, where we pray to the Mother of God every day. She'll accept you as her daughter, and you won't be orphaned anymore."

Her kindness only unleashed more tears. My body released its physical aches in a flood I didn't think would ever stop. Sor Berenguela went about her work in the garden and let me sit in the shade of a flowering shrub and weep.

My sorrow strengthened as I thought of how much I missed my mother, and of the way my father disappeared into himself when she died. He seemed to have drowned himself in tears, and couldn't have known what he was doing when he sold me. I couldn't hate him when Don Ordoño had turned out to be so generous. And there I was, because of the inexplicable actions of those two men, in the place where I'd always wanted to be. Until that moment, it had been more of a nightmare than a dream come true. But there had been Don Ordoño's extraordinary charity to me, and Teresa was doing her best to help me, and now Sor Berenguela showed me unexpected kindness. Maybe it was going to be all right. I felt I'd lived centuries over the course of the last day.

I breathed deeply. I was completely dry. I stood up and choked, "Thank you," to Sor Berenguela, who had her basket full of beets, melons, cucumbers, and carrots in different colors.

She waved so I would go to the other end of the garden with her. "Look here," she said. Against the wall, in the corner, a plant with thorns displayed the remains of bright red flowers with five petals. I would've known the fragrance anywhere.

"Roses," I sighed, leaning in to inhale.

"We don't really eat them, but maybe we could start to make perfume and rose water for the rich people who come to the convent. When the abbess finds out these are here, I'm just going to tell her we need them because they're St. Mary's flower."

"Rose of all roses, flower of all flowers," I sang.

"My goodness," said Sor Berenguela. "We'll have to get you into the choir."

We delivered the full basket to the kitchen, where the nuns who cooked received it enthusiastically. Sor Berenguela gave me more credit than I deserved for finding the beets and carrots that were ready to pluck. During the office of Terce, I listened hard. I didn't understand Latin, but it was easy enough to pick out the name of the Glorious Virgin, which was also my name.

Before I had time to tell anyone that I felt like I was in the right place at last, another dour-looking nun took me out to the forest to gather and cut firewood. I'd only ever seen my father do such work before, so I knew it must be laborious, but it was worse than I could've imagined. Stooping, bending, lifting heavy trunks, then getting blisters on my palms from swinging the axe with enough force, time after time. The nun didn't help, only told me what to do, and that I was doing it badly. My body, already pushed to its limits, went numb. I dared not compare my tasks with the suffering of Our Savior, but even so, I couldn't help but wonder when the torture would be over. The sun climbed the sky so slowly! At least this nun permitted me to take off my veil, which helped the arms I could hardly feel move more freely.

I finished chopping and started loading the wood into a cart I would probably have to draw by myself back to the kitchen. "Why don't the monks from the other side of the abbey help with this?" I asked, panting. "Surely it would be easier for them, and they wouldn't make as many mistakes as a novice like me."

More quickly than I thought possible, she snapped a branch off the tree where she was seated and struck me across the behind with it. I yelped at its sting, so different from my other pains.

"The abbess said you were no good." She remained standing at my side, flicking the switch in a wordless threat.

I understood I wasn't going to be able to share my thoughts with this nun. I'd hardly seen the abbess, and yet she seemed to have eyes on me at all times. I kept my prayers for the Sext bells to ring inside my collar. When they did, I curtsied rather than saying anything that might provoke her.

I headed to the well before the liturgy, intending to wash up a little, but the mere touch of the rope on my blisters nearly made me scream. I trembled, gazing at my destroyed hands, until Sor Catalina saw me and beckoned me into the church. I stood between her and Teresa and selfishly prayed for the strength to endure.

During the midday meal, I drew my veil close to my face and tried to deflect Abbess Blanche's gaze. I shoveled bread and vegetables into my mouth to the rhythm of the reader and was a little startled when Sor Catalina tapped me on the shoulder.

"You're coming with me now. I hear you need to learn to read."

I couldn't imagine what she meant, and was surprised to end up in the study where Don Ordoño had given the abbess his sapphire ring. My gaze darted around the room, but Abbess Blanche wasn't there. Sor Catalina took her place behind the lectern she'd been working at the day before while I looked on blankly.

"Sor Berenguela tells me you have a talent for gardening and a fine singing voice. Allowing you time to learn the liturgy and practice with the choir would lessen the physical labors of your day while using your true talent to praise God and His Mother. But I think we have to wait a while to propose it to Abbess Blanche. For now, Sor Berenguela is going to tell her you misbehaved terribly and must be punished with plenty of hours in the garden."

I took her ink-stained hand and kissed it. "Thank you. It means so much to me to work in the garden."

"I'm glad. Here, you're going to learn to read. There are many books on the plants God intends us to care for. Reading will also help you remember the melodies when you're singing in the choir."

On a long scrap of parchment that looked like it had been trimmed from a much larger sheet, Sor Catalina drew the word "pater." She pronounced the word and each of the letters, and I repeated after her until she was satisfied. The next word was "noster," and I enjoyed finding the same letters used in a different word. It was like magic. After several words, it dawned on me that she was writing out the Lord's Prayer.

"Oh! Teach me to read Ave Maria!" I exclaimed.

Sor Catalina chuckled. "We'll get there soon enough. You seem to be a ready pupil."

Abbess Blanche loomed in the doorway. Her presence put an end to our ease.

"A ready pupil?" she said, gliding to her desk. "Have we become a free school for delinquent girls?"

I chafed at the injustice coming out of her mouth, and was about to protest, but luckily, the bells rang for Nones. Sor Catalina and I nodded to the abbess and left for the church.

During the liturgy, Sor Catalina showed me the prayers we had to say, and I searched out the letters and words I'd just learned. It was a good distraction, as that way, I didn't have to look at the abbess presiding over the main altar.

Afterward, one of the nuns who always accompanied the abbess told me that I would be cleaning, this time starting in the cloister. My muscles clenched painfully just picking up the nearly empty bucket, but when I pulled it back out of the well full and turned around, I saw that there were several other nuns with cleaning rags waiting to fill their buckets, too. They told me their strategy to get the cloister and all the hallways done in time for Vespers. With several hours between offices and their cheerful encouragement, we had it done in plenty of time to wash up and rest quietly in the cloister for a few minutes. If the abbess thought this would punish me, she would have to think of something else.

After Vespers, I found Teresa, and we ate the evening meal together in near silence because I was exhausted. I was unmoved by the office of Compline, barely hearing anything. Then, I wanted to collapse on my cot, sure I would fall asleep immediately in spite of the aches that would be magnified by the hard surface. Teresa chose that moment to tell me she'd found a few lengths of blue cloth.

"We should at least get started on your habit. The abbess won't let you get by with that one for long."

She laid the fabric, some thread, and a needle in my lap. In the low light, I couldn't tell which piece was intended to go where. After only a moment, I folded the pieces back up. "There must be a simpler way to make a novice habit." A groan escaped me from deep down.

Teresa took the materials from me and arranged them on her bed. "I'll tack the pieces together with pins so you can see how to do it," she said before I lost consciousness.

Over the next few days, I stole daylight hours whenever I finished with a task to sew my habit. It came together quickly. Abbess Blanche didn't seem to notice the difference when I started wearing it Thursday morning, which I took as a sign of acceptance.

In addition to many of the same tasks as the first day, I toiled with goats, who took great pleasure in kicking and nipping at me, and at the bread ovens, which although they were outside, made for infernally hot work. I took special care making sure no nun burned herself, and developed a talent for taking the loaves out at the right moment according to their position in the oven.

On Thursday at midday, the abbess praised an especially

successful rye loaf. Hearing her words, I turned on the bench to see the abbess's table.

"It's wonderfully crisp and chewy, isn't it?" said the favored nun at her right. "It was made by the new novice, María."

Abbess Blanche grimaced. She couldn't seem to decide whether to spit out the morsel in her mouth or gag it down. She stared at me and finally swallowed.

"María!" Her voice echoed off the walls. The reader stopped her droning.

I stood and marched to the head table. Without a word, the abbess gripped my arm and headed with me back to her study. It was where I was to go next, anyway, for my reading lesson, so I had some hope Sor Catarina would follow us soon.

"Where is this guardian of yours?" The abbess rummaged among the shelves. "I'm starting to think he wanted to be rid of you and leave you here without paying any dowry at all."

"I think the tournament lasts a week, and I haven't been here seven days yet," I had time to say. Then she found what she'd been looking for: the long stick with the slightly filed edge for impressing straight lines into a page before writing the text. She stepped deliberately toward me, and I backed unconsciously into the other lectern.

"Didn't the sapphire ring buy me a week at least?" I pleaded. I knew in my heart that Don Ordoño would make good on his promise, but it would be for nothing if the abbess took the dowry from my flesh before he had the chance.

Her eyes darted to the coffer on the table. She couldn't resist opening it to gaze upon the ring and her other treasures. I eyed the door, wondering if I could slip out, but Sor Catalina walked in.

"Abbess, you have that meeting with the bishop to attend," she said with a curtsy.

"Thank you for reminding me, Sor Catalina." Abbess Blanche pursed her lips at me and sighed, closing the coffer. She replaced the rule on the shelf and told us to carry on as she left.

I held Sor Catalina to me, trying to stop my fear from pouring out of me. "Am I so bad?"

"Of course you aren't," said Sor Catalina, patting my veil the way my mother used to stroke my hair. "Abbess Blanche comes from a very noble family, and she has trouble with the vow of poverty she was obliged to take to enter our order." She pulled me apart from her to look into my eyes. "Your guardian will return soon, won't he?"

I wiped my tears and inhaled deeply. "As soon as the tournament is over. Have no doubt."

I continued trying my best at every task, but at the ovens, for example, I told the nuns that it would be better not to mention me to the abbess, whether it was for praise or not. Teresa helped me start another habit for when I needed to wash the first one. My muscles were already accustomed to the hardest work the abbess put me to, and during offices, I never missed a chance to pray for Don Ordoño to lift me out of the earthly purgatory of my hiding soon. The entire abbey buzzed with different speculations about what had happened to him or if he really would keep his promise, and I had to repeat, "Of course he will," in passageways and the cloister.

By Sunday night, I felt I'd lived at the abbey for more than a year. I was especially tired because I'd attended St. Mary's midnight Vigil offices the night before. If only I didn't have to focus on avoiding Abbess Blanche so much, I would've felt more at home at the abbey, praising St. Mary the way my mother always said I should, than I had back at home with my father and his sadness. I went to sleep wondering if the money from my sale had helped the state of his spirit or, more likely, brought him lower.

In dreams, I stood in an open field not unlike the one where I'd been tending my mother's garden when Don Ordoño showed up that fateful day. A ball of gleaming white light fell from the sky and grew to the size of a human on the horizon. It moved toward me placidly, and I wanted to run to it, but my feet couldn't leave the grasses and fading wildflowers.

Finally, the light faded, and the Mother of God stood before me. She took my hand.

"The fate of that knight is not fearful, for he now lives a perfect and holy life."

Her voice must've had the power to put pictures in my mind, for I saw Don Ordoño at the heavenly banquet with all the saints. My heart filled with gladness to see him there, but also with sorrow for me, for I knew he must be dead and could never bring my dowry.

The Most Glorious Virgin continued. "You are to deliver my message to the abbess carefully. She must hurry to the place where the knights fought, for in that spot they killed and buried that man and took him from this bitter and barren life. She will be certain of the place when she sees a beautiful rose blooming."

In my mind, a single red rose blossomed on a loose mound that must've been near the tournament grounds. Dew drops glistened on the petals in the morning sunlight. Don Ordoño's enemies must have killed him and disposed of his body disrespectfully, but St. Mary marked the spot with her rose so the abbess could find it and give him a proper burial in our convent.

"She must not object, but go there joyfully," said the Most Gracious Queen.

I woke. I could feel my heartbeat in every corner of my body. I felt in the pit of my stomach that because Don Ordoño no longer had the sapphire ring with him, it had cost him victory and brought about the treachery of his enemies. He had done no less than die for me. I worried that his death meant I'd have to leave the abbey, but it wasn't for me to disobey a direct order from the Queen of Heaven. I must deliver her message, whatever the cost.

I reached for my habit in the dark and pulled it over my chemise for modesty, but couldn't find my collar or coif. "What are you doing?" came Teresa's voice as I closed our cell door behind me.

There was little more light in the passageways, and even when I found the columns of the cloister, no moonlight showed the way. A dying torch on the wall outside the church acted as a beacon, and I found Abbess Blanche's study door, shut tight.

I leaned against the wall and slid down to wait. It couldn't be long until Matins, and the abbess would probably stop in her study to find the right hymnal or to finger her treasures. I dared not seek out her cell. Being there outside my schedule, without my veil, and not having met her eye for several days was probably enough to send her into a punishing frenzy. I mustn't forget the Blessed Virgin's exact message. I must stay awake and meet the abbess with the power of the Celestial Queen buoying my own strength.

I woke when Abbess Blanche kicked me in the gut.

"Wait!" I cried over the last tolling of the bells. "I have an important message from the Virgin Mother. She brings news of Don Ordoño!"

"St. Mary spoke to you?" Though her face was shaded by the weak morning light behind her, the abbess's skepticism was plain.

"She held my hand and told me Don Ordoño has been

killed and buried near the tournament grounds." I sat up and remained on my knees, folding my hands to plead humbly. "You're to disinter him and bring his body here for an honorable burial. You'll find him in a mound with St. Mary's red rose in full bloom even though the season for roses is nearly past."

"Whoever heard or saw such a thing? You must think me very stupid and hasty. I won't go there for you."

"The Mother of God told me you must go, and joyfully."

"Liar. Go put your collar and veil on before I kick you again." She stamped her foot and put her key to the lock. "And don't be late for Matins."

I stumbled across the cloister and through the passageways, which were full of nuns headed to Matins. I came upon my cell door, but before I could open it to get my collar and headpiece, St. Mary appeared between me and the door and grasped my shoulders. I felt her fingers like the talons of a hawk, and her eyes burned with heavenly blue fire.

"Go back to that bold, haughty, and scornful abbess and inform her that I know of the grave mortal sins she's committed." Nuns filed around us as if the Mother of God wasn't there. "The abbess should go to terrible perdition, for she has committed sins like a vile wretch."

St. Mary disappeared, but I was left with images in my mind of abhorrent sins of the flesh I would've preferred never to contemplate. I stood there, frozen, until all the nuns had passed by. Then I picked up the skirt of my habit, ran down the corridor, and cut through the cloister.

The abbess was locking the door of her study. I slid across the polished floor and knelt, taking her hand in supplication.

"What are you doing, girl, without your veil?" She tried to throw me off, but I held fast.

"St. Mary has another message for you," I whispered, not daring to look the abbess in the eye.

"More of this nonsense?" Abbess Blanche scoffed.

I forced the words through the fear that nearly closed my throat. "The Queen of Heaven says she knows that not only do you not keep your vow of poverty, accepting coins and jewels and keeping them in your coffers for your own pleasure, but you also break your vow of chastity with the sacristan on the other side of the abbey while the rest of us are working."

With superhuman force, the abbess threw me into the corner, but then stood silently.

"If you don't find Don Ordoño and bring him back here, St. Mary will be very displeased," I said, not to threaten her, but because I knew it to be true.

She stared at me as if she'd never seen me before. She stepped away down the corridor woodenly, picking up her pace on the other end of the cloister. I didn't have to wonder where she was headed.

I sped through the church, twisting my hair up as I entered the sacristy. Several nuns who awaited the abbess looked at me expectantly. I fell to my knees.

"The abbess has an urgent errand. She won't be joining us for Matins," I whispered into my clasped hands.

"Very well, then," said one nun, who put her hand on my shoulder to have me rise to my feet. The other nuns filed out to the main altar, and the one who'd spoken pulled an altar cloth out of one of the smaller drawers and covered my head with it. "After prayers, and before you go to help the cooks in the kitchen, find your collar, coif, and veil, and tidy your hair properly."

She gave me a pat on the bottom as if I were a naughty child, and I scurried gratefully into the nave to find Teresa. I knew the Matins prayers by heart, and I enjoyed the office in spite of myself. I felt ashamed to discover how little I missed the abbess.

Abbess Blanche didn't arrive in time for Lauds, or Prime, or breakfast. After I had told Sor Berenguela what had happened, and we were watering the celery, Sor Catalina appeared at the garden gate, breathless.

"The abbess has returned from her errand and wants us all to assemble in the courtyard." She turned and skittered back without waiting for us to clean our hands of garden soil.

Every nun in the abbey, some hundred souls, crowded the courtyard. I slipped between keyrings, elbows, and shoulders to take a place at the front of the audience, for the abbess was holding forth as if giving the greatest sermon.

"It was just as St. Mary had foretold: a red rose in full bloom, glistening with morning dew, atop a mound with no other flowers. An inappropriately lonely resting place for someone so favored by the Virgin Mother. I went into the city, to where they were setting up the market. With the help of a farmer, I disinterred the knight and brought him here in the farmer's wheelbarrow to be buried with honors."

A rumble of awe spread through the assembly.

"But how did you know what St. Mary said?" came the innocent question from a nun I still hadn't met. "Did she tell you herself?"

The abbess's mouth worked to find words that skirted the line between falsehood and truth, but found none. Her gaze landed on me, surely against her will.

"The new novice?" said the questioning nun.

Sor Berenguela pushed through the crowd from where she started at the back and declared, "Yes! María told me all about her vision of the Blessed Virgin and her instructions to the abbess."

Everyone's gaze was on me, and I shrank humbly, unable to think.

"Where is the body?" asked Sor Catalina helpfully.

"With the farmer, in the morgue," said the abbess.

As one, the group of a hundred nuns entered the passageway and filed out the back of the abbey to the small building where bodies were prepared for placement in sarcophagi. I didn't enter the building, but waited with Teresa and Sor Catalina for a couple of monks from the other side of the abbey to carry Don Ordoño out on a plank.

A light linen cloth covered his entire body, but I knew the shape of the man who had nearly ruined me, then ended up doing his best to save me. The fabric outlined his nose and sank onto his eyelids. My heart clenched to see the useless shell, such a dreadful contrast with the image St. Mary had shown me of Don Ordoño hale and bright at the heavenly banquet.

They laid the body carefully in a marble sarcophagus fit for a king. The abbot said many prayers in Latin, and six monks sang what I hoped was a prayer for Don Ordoño's soul. With a system of ropes and wheelworks and a lot of muscle, the monks fitted a marble slab over the top of the sarcophagus. There Don Ordoño would stay until he was nothing but bones. I made up my mind to place red roses atop that stone whenever they were in bloom. Many years in the future, when the bones were transferred to a niche, I would continue to put roses next to Don Ordoño for the rest of my life, commemorating his noble sacrifice for my sake.

A few days later, I paced the cloister outside the chapterhouse while the noblest nuns in the abbey debated my fate. I could hear murmurs through the arched window. Sor Catalina and

Sor Berenguela defended me passionately against the only objector, Abbess Blanche. No one else could reasonably deny the evidence.

Finally, the council flowed out of the chapterhouse. Each one clasped my hands and said things like, "Congratulations," or, if they'd worked with me, "You deserve this."

The abbess didn't stop, but nodded at me wordlessly. Then I was sure she could no longer threaten my body, my soul, or my place at this abbey. I was already grinning when Sor Catalina and Sor Berenguela closed the chapterhouse door behind them.

Sor Catalina engulfed me in her arms, and when she let go, Sor Berenguela had her turn.

"It's been decided that you are no ordinary novice," said Sor Berenguela. "Your dowry has been paid with the sapphire ring, which will soon decorate the hand of the image of Our Lady on the main altar."

I exhaled with tremendous relief, and a picture came into my mind of the sapphire matching the statue's eyes perfectly.

"And as an extraordinary novice," said Sor Catalina, "the council has decided that you need more time for contemplation to put your powerful prayers to work for the good of the abbey and all Christendom. You'll be allowed to choose the labors that least interfere with your divine purpose."

"Oh!" I shouted. The noise comically echoed off the columns and arches. "I choose to spend more time close to the Mother of God in her garden with Sor Berenguela, and to spend many hours every day with you, Sor Catalina, so you can help me write my story for all to know in the future."

"And what's more," continued Sor Berenguela, "since you have this connection with St. Mary, we're going to let the Queen of

Heaven decide when you should be allowed to take your vows
and become a nun of this abbey. Let us know what she tells you."
She winked.

I laughed with my whole body. I had a feeling it would be very
soon indeed.

The Right Revenge

Cantiga 207

Zamora, Spain, thirteenth century

ortún paused at the golden stone threshold of his church, New Saint Mary, and took his wife's hand. Aminta's hem fell out of her grasp to the straw-covered floor, and they passed under the horseshoe archway to dip their hands into the holy water and cross themselves. As his eyes adjusted to the candlelight, Fortún scanned the crowd gathered for morning mass for any sign of his son.

The boy—well, he was a man now, knighted two years before with three successful campaigns against the Benimerin Moors from Africa—sometimes stayed out all night. But he'd always come to morning mass, no matter what revels or ruckus he'd had to abandon.

"Where's Pedro? I was sure he'd be here already," said Aminta. "He's even more devoted to the Blessed Virgin than we are."

"He'll be along soon," Fortún said, though what he really

wanted was to search the entire city until he found his boy.

Perhaps Pedro would smile sheepishly about his tardiness and present his father with a basket full of trout he'd caught instead. Or he'd come upon Pedro in the street, leading home a horse he'd won at cards in the tavern. But no, Pedro wouldn't miss Mary's mass for anything so frivolous. Two weeks in Pedro's entire life, he'd stayed home from New Saint Mary, and it was because he'd broken his leg during training. As soon as he could make his way with a crutch, there he was, in the front row, half-kneeling awkwardly but with all the devoutness his mother and father had taught him.

It was strange to stand next to the other worshippers and face the walls painted in blue and red with scenes from the life of St. Mary without Pedro. Lords and peasants alike openly stared at the couple, taking in the obvious absence, until the priest came out from the sacristy and led them in the first prayers. Fortún glanced behind him to see if perhaps Pedro had slipped inside the church. He hadn't, and his father stumbled on his way to the altar to take communion.

Heaving a sigh, Fortún gazed upon on the image of St. Mary that presided over the altar. Her placid expression radiated a light that warmed his heart and gave him the strength to return to his spot at the front of the nave. When Aminta joined him, he squeezed her hand.

"We'll find him after mass," he whispered. The choir's voices echoed off the walls and filled their ears, but she gave him a nervous smile to show she'd heard.

They didn't dwell in the church chatting with their neighbors. They had just opened the door when they saw the tanner's son running up the street toward them.

"Don Fortún, Doña Aminta, come quick. It's Pedro, he's

outside the church in the Olivares quarter!" The boy's gangly legs carried him back in the direction he'd come from.

"What do you mean?" Aminta shouted after him.

He turned around at the opening to Butchers Street. "He's been wounded! Come quick!"

Fortún grasped Aminta's hand, and they followed the boy. The stench from the butchers' shops assaulted them as soon as they left the church plaza to enter the tunnel-like street. Fortún swerved around tables and carts. He splashed through the red swill on the ground. He couldn't see anything, couldn't imagine what had happened to his son. His wife struggled to maneuver while holding her skirts over the street's quickening current.

"Go ahead," said Aminta. "I'll catch up."

Fortún sped down the street, passing the butchers and even the tanner's son. He dashed through the thick stone city wall at St. Martin's Gate and made it down the slope without stumbling. He ran free of obstacles in the fields below the city, hugging the curve of the wall as it rose higher and higher above him. The distance had never seemed so great, in spite of his hurry. When the castle loomed overhead, he wondered if his heart would give out. Then he wished it had.

It would have been better to die without seeing Pedro's powerful body prone on the ground like so much garbage, unable to defend himself from the crows that were circling menacingly overhead, dipping between the buildings and cawing their perverse song. Pedro's arms were splayed to his sides, his dark hair matted with blood against his head. His jaw hung open as if frozen, gasping for air.

Fortún knelt at his son's unresponsive head and felt Pedro's blood soak through his hose to his knees. Pedro's tunic was limp fabric holding together gash after gash. His eyes, which had seen his mother's joy, his father's pride, so many strong enemies, and so many blessings from the Virgin Mary, stared upward, unseeing. Fortún placed his hand over Pedro's face and closed the useless eyelids.

The tanner's son came running.

"Wounded?" raged Fortún. "You call this wounded?" He lunged at the boy and grabbed his collar, shaking him by the neck. "My Pedro is dead. Dead! Who did this? Did you see who did this? Tell me!"

The boy wrenched out of his grasp. "It wasn't me! I only arrived in time to see Blas, the knight from Toro, running away."

"In which direction—" Fortún started, but a shriek from down the street rent his ears. "No, Aminta, darling, don't look!" He lurched toward his wife to catch her in his arms, but she shoved him out of her way. She hunched over her son and kissed his face, covering it in tears.

The boy stood with Fortún, frozen in place. "Go fetch the judge and our priest from New Saint Mary," he ordered the boy. "Tell them exactly what's happened, not the nonsense about wounding you told us."

Once the boy had run off, Aminta lay down alongside her son in the packed earth street and rocked slowly back and forth. Her skirts covered both their legs like a blanket, but Pedro's wounds still glistened in the sunlight. Fortún couldn't bear to look.

He turned his gaze upward, where he saw the strong city wall, and behind it, the rectangular, stalwart cathedral bell tower, which served as a watchtower and, in the worst cases, a place from which to hurl lances and other objects. The golden stones had defended Zamora for hundreds of years. Nothing could break them. But they hadn't protected his son. What were they good for?

•   •   •

After the funeral mass, Pedro's shrouded body was sealed into a sarcophagus in the churchyard outside New Saint Mary. In time, his bones would lie under the floor near the altar where Fortún had taken comfort just before his life had stopped making sense.

In the four months since, no one had seen the murderer Don Blas, even though the judge had placed men at every city gate to watch for him. Fortún himself had made the trip to Toro. He asked everyone he saw, in the plaza, at the collegiate church, in the market, near the fortress, and none gave any notice of the killer. Back in Zamora, Fortún visited every gate in the city wall at least once per day to ask the guards if they'd seen anything.

The one place he hadn't returned to was St. Mary's church. Mary hadn't cared for Pedro's devotion, or Fortún's, or Aminta's, in spite of the masses they'd attended and paid for over so many years. It was the only explanation. Why else would she have let Pedro die? Fortún no longer dignified her church with his attendance.

Fortún invited Aminta's sister to live with them to alleviate the silence and bring some kind of life back into the house. The two women did chores quietly and made food no one ate. Unlike Pedro's father, they hadn't lost their devotion, and left every day to attend mass. Fortún couldn't bear the silence during those hours, so the house stood empty as he wandered the streets, shunning well-meaning neighbors, searching faces for that of his son's killer.

He had only seen Don Blas once or twice from a distance, but he was convinced he would know the man by the sense of evil that surely lurked behind his eyes. Killing Pedro would have left an indelible mark, and by that sign, Fortún would know where to take his revenge.

His only sense of the passing days came from his ideas for tortures to exact on Don Blas. If Fortún found him on a Monday, he would tie Don Blas to two horses and set them running in opposite directions. He would leave the armless assailant to bleed to death on the street, just as Pedro had. If the fated day were a Tuesday, Don Blas would be hanged from a tree in Val de Oro Woods, gasping for life in a sorry imitation of Fortún's struggle to understand why Pedro had to suffer when he'd been so good and devout. A Wednesday would require an executioner's axe. Fortún envisioned the vicious pleasure it would give him to toss the lifeless head of his enemy from the castle so it could roll in the fields below and curdle under a sun that relentlessly rose over a world without Pedro. On a Thursday, Fortún would ask the Lord of Zamora not to feed his hunting hounds for a week or two in order to give them the delight of tearing the unrepentant felon limb from limb until the murderer was nothing more than canine excrement. If Fortún met Blas on a Friday, he would tie the shameless criminal down and slice out his heart with a butcher's knife. He would gag the killer so that he had to choke on his own screams of pain and terror, exactly the way Fortún did every day. Moments before dying, Blas would understand something of the pain he'd caused Pedro's family. It would have to suffice.

One cold winter day, Fortún wrapped himself up in his cloak and checked with the guards at Bishop's Gate, Traitor's Gate, Market Gate, and St. Martin's Gate, making his regular rounds. That day was different because he didn't think he saw Blas stalking him in every corner, underneath every man's cap.

The mayor's son, a friend of Pedro's, greeted him on the way to New Saint Mary, and Fortún didn't feel the need to avoid his gaze. He wondered what could be so different as he walked. At Fair Gate, he spoke at length with the guards, but they had neither seen nor heard anything that would make this day different than any other. He thanked them and continued along the long stretch of wall with no gates. As he got closer to St. Torquatus Gate, his pulse raced. He didn't know why until he rounded the corner.

The guards at St. Torquatus had tied a man by the wrists and ankles and held him between them, each receiving an equal share of the knees and elbows that struggled against the bindings. Fortún tried to look into the man's eyes. Was Pedro's death written there?

"Don Fortún, we've got him," said one of the guards.

"This is Don Blas from Toro?" said Fortún. His previous sightings from afar were no help. He wouldn't have recognized this man even if he'd walked up and introduced himself.

"He came barging right up to the gate as if he were the most innocent of men," said the other guard. "But don't worry, we got him for you. He's all yours."

Fortún grasped the cord leading from the man's wrists and yanked, forcing the prisoner closer. Blas's eyes were practically shut in his grimace, but this must be the man who'd killed Pedro. Fortún nodded. Blas's lips curled with disdain, then spat a wine-soaked glob that landed on Fortún's nose. It was the sign he needed. He pulled on the cord, and the prisoner was obliged to follow.

It was Saturday. He hadn't prepared a vengeance for a Saturday. The right thing to do would be to take the murderer to where Pedro had died and stab him in the same spot, with his eating knife, if that was all he had. He headed to St. Martin's Gate, following the same route he'd taken the day Pedro died. The prisoner stumbled constantly over the bindings at his ankles and yelled over and over again, "Where are you taking me?"

The noise attracted a crowd of merchants, servants, and children. Fortún knew Aminta was at mass, and it was just as well. She could learn the good news without having to witness the violence. The crowd recognized what was happening, and as they found stones or vegetables from stalls, they tossed them gleefully at Blas.

"What have I done?" shouted Blas. Dodging a stone directed at his head, he lost his balance at the gate and tumbled down the slope. Fortún ran to catch the cord, which had slipped from his grasp. He helped the man to his feet.

"What quarrel do I have with you?" asked Blas.

Fortún saw that he truly didn't know. He felt obliged to give the man a moment to reflect on his actions. "You killed my son, Pedro, didn't you?"

"Oh!" Blas's face opened up in surprise. "That was your son?"

Fortún took it as a confession. "I loved Pedro more than my own life. If someone had to die, it should've been me. Now you've condemned me to this shadow of a life I never wanted to live. I'm taking you to the place you killed my son to give you no more than you deserve, a death just like Pedro's."

Blas turned, pulled on the cord with a grunt, and fell to the ground again. He worked his legs in the snowmelt and mud, but couldn't stand up or run away. The crowd had come down the slope, and at Fortún's bidding, a butcher and his apprentice lifted the criminal and carried him behind Fortún's sure steps. He ignored the crowd's uproar and advanced toward the place of execution as if he'd practiced hundreds of times.

The wall and cathedral tower loomed over the church plaza in the Olivares quarter. To Fortún, the only difference from four months before was that snow buried the street where his son had lain.

The crowd trampled into the plaza, and the butchers set the prisoner on his feet. Fortún imagined clearly the way Blas would lie helpless, bleeding slowly in the cold. If the authorities didn't dispose of the body, it might still be there during Holy Week, silently declaiming the knight's unforgivable crime.

Fortún's gaze was drawn to the arch over the church door. Three layers of sculptures in a perfect semicircle portrayed all the Earth's known animals, the lush vines of Paradise, and twelve different human activities—a calendar of life and worldly concerns. In the center of the innermost arch, someone had recently carved out a new relief and painted the background sky blue while the main subject was whiter than the snow at their feet. A paschal lamb, an innocent for the slaughter, just like Pedro. Fortún felt compelled to walk inside.

"Is he going to kill him inside the church?" the butcher's apprentice asked.

"I don't think that's allowed," said the butcher. They followed Fortún with the prisoner and the rest crowded inside and filled the empty nave.

The church's niches were occupied by male saints, shepherds and farmers like the men who attended services. A priest came out of the sacristy with a candle nearly as tall as he. "Mass doesn't start for another hour," he said. "I don't know you. Who are all of you?"

The priest approached the butchers and the prisoner and they talked, but Fortún ignored them. He'd spotted what he hadn't known he was looking for.

In the corner near the sacristy, a small wooden image of St. Mary held her hands out as if asking something of Fortún, her one-time devotee. She was nothing like the image at the main altar of New Saint Mary. While that Mother of God sat upon a gilded throne with her Son on her lap, wearing a mild expression of heavenly contentment, this Mary stood alone, her forlorn face turned upward as if searching heaven. Pearl-like tears dotted her cheeks. She had lost her Son, and Fortún had never felt so connected to her.

His body opened into a torrent of shared grief. He fell to his knees before the Queen of Heaven. How could he have abandoned Mary, who understood his sorrow and Aminta's? Why had he blamed Mary for Pedro's death when the Blessed Mother would never inflict the pain she had suffered on any other parent?

"Forgive me, please, I beg you," he whispered. "I haven't carried my grief for Pedro following your example. What can I do to make it right?" He brushed the tears away with the sleeve of his tunic, and looking into Mary's desperate eyes, he understood.

Don Blas was also someone's son.

He turned to see the butchers arguing with the priest even as they held a struggling Don Blas between them. Fortún walked silently toward them, drawing his eating knife from his belt.

"No," shouted the priest. "You can't kill him here!"

Fortún knelt and slit the cord around Blas's ankles before anyone understood what he was doing. He took Blas's fists and flicked the knife through the binding at his wrists, and the prisoner was free. The priest and the crowd stood in silent astonishment, and Don Blas collapsed into the butcher's arms.

"Look!" A child pointed behind them, to the corner with the image of St. Mary.

The Blessed Mother had fallen to her knees and put her hands together in prayer. Fortún wasn't sure if his vision was cloudy, but she seemed to look straight at him. A woman's voice swept lightly through the nave, reaching every niche and archway in spite of its airiness.

"Thank you."

With a gentle nod, the image resumed its stance.

No-Man's-Land

Cantiga 233

Eastern border of Castile,
early eleventh century

Jacinto tilted his head and admired the stars. He closed his eyes to inhale the scent of the campfire and listen to his companions' booming laughter.

As on the previous two evenings, the thirty knights and their squires had broken bread with the monks of San Sebastián de Silos, heard Vespers mass, then returned to benches around an open fire near their tents with leather pouches of Rioja wine paid for with Moorish gold coins.

Jacinto wouldn't have minded if they did it exactly the same for another three nights, and another three after them. He was in the best company. Together, they could expand the frontiers of Castile all the way to the sea. After a good rest.

"You're not falling asleep on us, are you?" said Rodrigo with an elbow into Jacinto's side.

Jacinto guffawed to hide his reverie. "I can keep up with any of you."

"Ah, let him sleep," cried another knight. "He killed more Moors than all of us put together."

"It wasn't that many," said Jacinto.

"Stop being so modest," said their commander, Don Gerardo Martínez. He'd spent the previous nights in a private room in the monastery, and his knights hadn't seen him approaching in the dark. The entire company stood at his sudden appearance in the firelight.

"Lord," they said.

"Sit, sit, my soldiers. I declare, Don Jacinto," continued Don Gerardo, "that the squires witnessed all the action this last week, and they reported that you killed twenty-nine of our enemies, while your nearest comrade killed two. Most importantly, we sent the rest of those miscreants running back to Córdoba. Our duties now lie in repopulating the land with good Castilians who can establish farms, markets, and fortresses. Tomorrow morning, we leave for Burgos to enlist them."

"Back to my family!" exclaimed Rodrigo, slapping Jacinto's thigh while the other knights cheered and shouted.

"I'll see my wife again!"

"My children will come running to meet me!"

Jacinto remained silent. What business did he have any distance from the frontier? He had no family to return to. He couldn't bear the dithering about pacts and fealty in Burgos when the only solution to the problem of the Moorish incursions was to go out and fight them.

Was he expected to live on a farm? He pictured himself among radishes, his sword languishing in the ashes of the hearthside, away from the tumult, the clash of axes, the eye-to-eye confrontations where he had always prevailed, and knew he had nothing to offer the interior of the kingdom.

But they must bring landowners and merchants to the new border to take a firm hold, and those men and women wouldn't be safe armed only with hoes and hope.

"My lord, who's going to be *adelantado* of the frontier?" Jacinto asked. "I'd like to serve with him."

"What are you thinking?" whispered Rodrigo. "With all the honors and payment you've earned waiting for you in Burgos?"

"I'd like to guard the rightful homesteaders from attack."

"The king will appoint *adelantados* in due course," said Don Gerardo. Jacinto nodded, then hid his impatience staring into the flames. He passed the wineskin to Rodrigo absently, without taking a swig.

Amid the murmuring, some of the knights stood as if they would return to their tents. But Don Gerardo continued, "Before we make ready for departure tomorrow, I must ask a favor of one of you."

The popping of the fire was the only sound as the soldiers waited to attend their lord's wishes.

"I'm told the hermit monks at Peñacoba are copying and illuminating a Bible for the queen, but they've run out of parchment. I've purchased twenty sheets of goat vellum from the brothers here at San Sebastián and have promised before the Virgin Mary's altar that the hermits will receive them. Who will deliver the sheets for me? He should leave tomorrow and rejoin us in Burgos as quickly as he can."

A collective sigh assured Jacinto that none of his comrades wanted to delay their journey home. Don Gerardo clasped his hands together as if praying that one of them would change his mind.

"Where is this Peñacoba?" Jacinto asked with a smile his commander probably couldn't see.

Don Gerardo grinned with relief. "It's not far. From here, go south through Yecla Pass, then turn east, and within two hours you'll see it perched atop the rock."

It might be better to stay on the frontier, even without his comrades, and for only a little while longer, than to return to the city with them. The opportunity must've been made for Jacinto, and he should see where it led.

"It sounds like an easy journey. I'd be happy to help you keep your pledge, my lord."

"You would go south, toward the heathen armies, alone, with no one else, all by yourself?" Rodrigo asked.

"If you're so worried about it, go with him," heckled a soldier on the other side of the fire.

"No, Don Rodrigo is right," said Don Gerardo. "Although the hermitage isn't very close to where we've been fighting, it would be foolish to head out alone. Will anyone go with Don Jacinto to meet with whatever the road brings, together?"

After many moments of whispers and grumbling around the fire, Rodrigo looked Jacinto in the eye. "I'm sorry, my friend. My home is calling to me. But take my squire, Pelayo. He'll make sure no harm comes to you. No one wants to get home safely more than he does."

The squire stood up from his seat on the other side of Rodrigo and folded his arms. Before he could speak, Rodrigo continued, "Don't think of refusing, Pelayo. I'm sending you because I know you can do it well, and Jacinto is my best friend. Do me this favor, and I'll honor you with gold and a title when you come back to Burgos."

The squire huffed, then nodded. "I'll do it for my wife's sake.

She thought this campaign would bring us fortune for our children. But I do it only for them."

"Thank you, Don Rodrigo, and thank you, Pelayo. Your sacrifice will not go unnoticed," said Don Gerardo. "We'll all go to mass at sunrise. Be ready to leave afterward."

Once they'd packed everything into the carts except the tents and what they would need in the morning, the soldiers rolled out their beds, their arms and armor within easy reach. Most in Jacinto's tent were snoring, surely enjoying dreams of home.

But Jacinto shifted uncomfortably on the straw and blankets even though he had no wounds to ail him. The hour was late and packing up had taken what was left of his strength, and still sleep refused to come. Pelayo had a family waiting for him, but no one waited for Jacinto. Pelayo was on the frontier to earn gold and a title and return home, but Jacinto felt most at home on the frontier. Who was right?

Pelayo lay next to him, and Jacinto thought he could feel the squire's gaze on him all night.

In the morning, after mass, Jacinto stopped before the Blessed Virgin's altar. As the other knights filed past, he raised his hands in supplication before her benevolent gaze and whispered.

"Blessed Mother, you might expect me to ask for a successful journey. I do, but I also ask that you show me your Son's plan for me as I ride toward your hermitage. I don't think there is a place for me in Burgos. I have served you well on the frontier, killing many men of false religion who want to steal back the land we've won for your sake. Perhaps I've killed too many. Maybe you would rather I captured some of them for ransom or peace negotiations, Most Serene Virgin. But killing is all I know. Would you really have me plant radishes? I can do so much more for your glory. You, for whom anything is possible, please show me what you want me to do."

By the time he came out of the church, most of the soldiers had already saddled up.

"I didn't let anyone take your horse," said Rodrigo, handing Jacinto the chestnut's reins. "You rode him throughout the campaign and he never failed you. He'll carry you well. And after all, it's only a short distance farther than the rest of us are going, and then you're coming back to us."

"Thank you, my friend. Having Mistral will be almost like having you at my side," said Jacinto.

If it was such a short distance, why shouldn't Rodrigo come along, after all? They could make believe they were still on the campaign, laugh and sing until they caught up with the rest of the company.

"Don't forget Pelayo. He'll be there, too." Rodrigo said with a wince, as if he'd heard Jacinto's thoughts and regretted not being a more loyal friend.

Don Gerardo emerged from the crowd with Pelayo, who carried the twenty sheets of vellum draped over his arm. With only a nod at Jacinto, the squire folded the precious pages into Jacinto's saddlebag.

"I can never repay you for this unselfish act," Don Gerardo said. "But I will certainly try when you return to us."

"Thank you, my lord, but it's no imposition. I need to make a pilgrimage in any case," said Jacinto. He hoped the Virgin Mary would understand the detour as a pilgrimage and grant him the gift he'd asked for in return.

The company and Jacinto wished each other safe journeys and headed in opposite directions. Pelayo followed their southern route far behind Jacinto, setting his horse to a pace slower than the quietest meandering stream.

"Come on, trembler," said Jacinto. "Half the monasteries around here are named St. Pelayo. You can't possibly come to any harm with so many namesake protectors."

"We're riding away from my patrons, right into the mouth of the enemy."

"No. Remember where we've been fighting? To the east." At least, Jacinto didn't think the hermitage would exist inside disputed lands. Don Gerardo had assured them of it. "There's nothing to the south of Castile. Nothing for days."

"Certainly, and there are no St. Jacinto churches, either, anywhere near here. Who's protecting you?"

"I'm told Peñacoba is St. Mary's hermitage. There is no greater protector than the Mother of God."

Jacinto felt the warmth of the Blessed Virgin's mantle as she watched over them. They settled into a comfortable pace. Sparrows chirruped to each other, then darted under the cover of the scrub. A vulture circling overhead traced black shadows over Jacinto's path. Soon enough, the silent grey stone of Yecla Pass towered over them on either side.

Jacinto wondered if the Virgin Mary could watch over them now. Could she see them through so much rock?

"I think I saw movement on the mountaintop," Pelayo whispered, so low Jacinto could hardly hear him.

"It was probably deer," said Jacinto. But it could also be lynxes or bears or even a dragon disturbed from its slumber by their pass through the mountain.

"No, no," whispered Pelayo even lower. "I think it was a scout. I hear sounds echoing off the canyon walls, sounds of hoofs on stone and swords unsheathed. Sounds of men."

Jacinto was concentrating so hard on understanding Pelayo that when his horse's hoof kicked a pebble in the trail, it sounded like a thunderclap. When Pelayo next spoke, Jacinto could barely hear him over his heart pounding in his ears.

"How many Moors did you kill during this campaign?" the squire asked.

Jacinto swallowed. He knew what Pelayo meant. "Some say as many as thirty, but I don't think it was that many."

"Thirty reasons for someone who knew a Moorish warrior to make a special trip into these mountains." Pelayo was no longer whispering.

A revenge mission wouldn't need a territory to claim or call for a commander. A revenge mission needed only a dead friend or brother. Jacinto remained quiet. He thought he could hear men, too.

But they were nearly out of the pass. Even if they kept this same pace, it would only be a few minutes before they turned east, and they might be able to see Peñacoba between the hills within the hour. If anyone wanted revenge, he would have to take it soon.

"Stay back!" shouted Pelayo.

Jacinto looked behind him. An army of mounted Moorish soldiers, their jeweled turbans glittering as much as their curved swords, bore down on Pelayo—on Jacinto, with all the clamor of the hounds of Hell.

Where had they come from? Jacinto pulled the reins and squeezed Mistral with his legs, but the horse spun in place, too intelligent to remain calm.

"I'm not with this man," cried Pelayo. "I don't even know him!"

The Moors swarmed around Pelayo, and Jacinto couldn't hear what was happening under the barking of their heathen language.

One, then two, then three, broke away from the group and turned their horses toward Jacinto. So outnumbered, no warrior of Castile would be stupid enough to wait for death. He didn't have to signal to his mount. They headed away through the pass, gaining speed and throwing dust behind them.

The pursuing warriors shouted something as their numbers grew. With repetition, Jacinto heard that they were speaking Latin for his benefit.

"You're going to die!" they yelled.

"You're going to die!" over and over, echoing off the ravine walls until Jacinto believed it was their multitude of words that would murder him.

Jacinto gasped for air. He urged his horse forward. They ran together in their panic, and with a last leap, they were beyond Yecla Pass. He yanked the rein to turn left. Mistral struggled, disoriented, but at last Jacinto was headed east. He looked over his shoulder and didn't see any of the warriors. They must still be in the pass, but he wasn't going back to find out.

The foothills swelled around him like baker's loaves, and Mistral was forced to slow to follow the curving path. The steed had already worked himself into a lather, but Jacinto pushed ever forward, the ululations of his enemies in his ears.

Leaning forward, sweat cascading down his face under his hardened leather helmet, Jacinto willed himself not to look back. When he did, sometimes he saw an empty path before a turn around a hillside, shrouded in leaning trees and tendrils, as dark as dusk in spite of the bright blue sky. Other times, all too often, he glimpsed the muzzle of the front stallion emerging from beyond the last bend, just as frantic to get ahead as his own.

In an open field, it might've been a matter of minutes before at least one of them caught up to him, and Jacinto praised the Blessed Virgin for having her hermitage in rocky terrain.

He and the horse worked together, coming down harder in the creaking saddle with every stride, twisting around hills with the same tawny grass, grey stones, and misshapen trees. All their effort escaped into a forward movement that wouldn't come. Somehow, they'd ended up on Fortune's wheel, rotating eternally to the same position, brought low by the infidels he'd thought he would always defeat in the name of God.

God and his Mother. He was riding toward them even now, when he felt most alone. Jacinto didn't know whether the hermits could help him.

Should he bring all this revenge and slaughter into a holy place? Had the Moors killed Pelayo? What would they do to the innocent monks?

Clutching at his heart, Jacinto looked ahead for some forking or switchback that might lead away from Peñacoba. But it was almost as if a giant serpent had lain in these foothills, creating a single depression. For all its twisting, there was nowhere else to go.

He closed his mouth and tried to swallow, but it was too dry. Pelayo had been carrying the wineskins.

Had Jacinto been right to leave Pelayo to an unspeakable fate? Shouldn't he have defended his friend's squire even to his own death?

"Add it to my sins, Glorious Mother," whispered Jacinto as he and Mistral turned yet another corner, "my multitude of sins, which I lay at your feet. I only ever committed sins while trying to serve you. Have mercy on my wretched life and beg your Son to forgive me."

Forgiveness was all he could hope for now. His enemies

might catch him at any moment and no one would ever know where his bones rested.

Atop the next hill, much closer than he could've dreamed, appeared a building with rounded sides made of golden stone and a bell suspended between two posts. In a gust of wind, the bell rang, thin in the noontime air, and for what seemed the first time, the sunlight illuminated the landscape, making the leaves on the trees and bushes shimmer.

"We're almost there," Jacinto said for Mistral to hear. The horse clambered through bushes and stopped at the foot of the hill, wheezing so heavily that Jacinto feared for his life. He looked back to see not only the lead horse, but three of his attackers and their mounts appearing from behind the nearest swell.

Jacinto's horse had carried him this far, but wouldn't be able to muster enough force in time. Knowing it might be his last decision on this Earth, he jumped to the ground, patted Mistral's flank in farewell, and willed his legs to carry him up the hill.

He threw down his helmet and fixed his gaze on the arched double door in the low, windowless building. He marched, mindless of the mounds of disturbed soil with wooden crosses nestled between the young fruit trees that flanked the path, breathing almost as hard as his horse behind him.

Jacinto pushed on the door with both hands. It gave way into a small chapel with a plain table covered in white silk as its altar. A monk was lighting beeswax candles around a wooden image of the Queen of Heaven. She wore a crown studded with sapphires and a blue robe embroidered with gold thread that glinted in the flickering light.

"In the name of the Virgin Mother, help me!" Jacinto tripped over his own foot and fell at the hem of the monk's black robe.

The monk threw his hands up in surprise, then scurried around Jacinto to slam the door and bar it shut.

Jacinto clasped his hands and looked into the eyes of the image from his place on the floor. Through cracked lips, he rasped, "Holy Mother of God, save me from these miscreants."

The monk disappeared behind a curtained doorway. Jacinto shut his eyes and squeezed out a tear.

"Sir Knight," the monk was saying above him. Jacinto opened his eyes, took the monk's proffered hand, and allowed himself to be led to a stone bench beside the main door. "Take this unconsecrated wine, traveler, and tell me what's happening."

Jacinto slumped in the seat, but gratefully took the wineskin and drained it before his breath returned to him.

"Brother Monk," he said at last. "My sins are so great that if the Blessed Virgin doesn't come to our aid, the men on their way here will kill me and you and all the other hermits and then profane your church. I'm sorry I brought their destruction here. I was on a mission to bring you vellum, but I'm such a sinner that even that noble purpose couldn't save me from my well-deserved fate. The avengers will steal my saddlebag and cast the pages to the wind."

The monk set his jaw, then took the empty wineskin from Jacinto's shaking hands. "Have faith, Sir Knight. You asked St. Mary to save you, and she never abandons those who call on her."

Jacinto wiped his face of the sweat, tears, and wine. "You're right, of course."

"How close behind you were they?" the monk asked.

"They should be here by now," Jacinto said, his hope renewed. "But I don't hear anything outside."

The monk screwed up his mouth. He unbarred the door

and opened it so that the tiniest sliver of sunlight entered the sanctuary. He crouched and held his face in the gap for a moment. With a smile Jacinto couldn't fathom, the monk opened the door wide, flooding the altar with light so that the Virgin's image appeared to nod at Jacinto.

The monk beckoned. Jacinto stood on knees that felt as if they were made of quince paste and leaned on the monk's shoulder as he squinted into the sunlight.

Atop the mounds of earth along the pathway and forming a line to block the doorway from attack waited an army. Or, not an army, but an assembly of forty or fifty knights from Castile, León, Navarra—all over Christian Hispania, judging by the riot of different colors and symbols on their coats of arms.

Each knight held drawn an old-fashioned sword of craftsmanship different than the one next to him, threatening Jacinto's former pursuers, who held their hands up in surrender. The Christians had been in battle already: covered with dust and sweat, some bled copiously from gashes in their chests, arms, or necks. A bearded knight wearing a white tunic with a red lion emblem nodded at Jacinto with a wink that only increased his bewilderment.

Jacinto witnessed the scene indistinctly through the soldiers standing in front of him, who had the consistency of smoke wafting from a campfire.

"It's the spirits of the men who died defending this land from the Moors and were buried here," said the monk. "The Blessed Virgin's own army is here to defend us."

Even with their diaphanous appearance, the soldiers cast steely gazes at the ten Moorish knights, who no longer looked proud despite their turbans and jewels. They hardly had the presence of mind to calm their panicky mounts.

"Glory to God and his Mother," whispered Jacinto, still not sure what he was seeing. Three other hermits joined them in the doorway to witness the miracle.

The enemy leader said something, and the party dismounted. The ghostly knights flickered but held their places. The Moorish knights gripped their weapons.

"Are they coming through?" Jacinto asked the monk. What could the spirits do to them, anyway? The hermitage was lost.

But after a few more words in that gruff language, the ten Moors threw their weapons to the ground. They approached the door with their hands held in front of them to show that they were empty. A ghostly knight stepped into their path, barring the way, but the Moors bowed low and then knelt. Their leader addressed the spirit so that Jacinto and the monk could hear.

"We see that you are not of this world, but we don't think your intentions are evil." The ghosts shook their heads, and the Moorish leader continued. "We honor you because you have been sent by Mary, mother of Jesus."

"They know the Blessed Virgin," interjected the monk.

"Because you defend this knight for her sake, we are prepared to pardon him, in spite of all the wrongs he has done us," said the leader. "If he is prepared to forgive us for attempting to avenge our relatives on him, we may part here as friends."

Jacinto looked back at the altar, and more than the sparkling crown or the gleaming robes, what caught his eye was St. Mary's face. It was probably carved of local wood and painted by one of the hermits, and it had held the same open half-smile ever since. But now it was a smile of approval, a smile that showed him the Blessed Virgin had not only saved him, but had also done as he'd asked by showing him how she wanted him to treat his enemies. Forgiveness washed over him like a cooling rain.

With tears in his eyes, Jacinto brushed through his smoky protectors and stood before the Moorish leader. At the bottom of the hill, he glimpsed Mistral, exhausted but unharmed and with his saddlebag undisturbed.

"First, I must know what's become of Pelayo. I saw you take him, but is he still alive?"

"The squire who surrendered to us? We left him in the pass. He wasn't our enemy, and we were running out of time to catch you. He probably headed back the way he came."

Jacinto smiled. Perhaps Pelayo would be reunited with Rodrigo that evening. What would Rodrigo say to the squire about how well he'd taken care of his best friend?

Jacinto held his hand out to the leader. "If you pardon me, then I am forgiven by none other than the Virgin Mother you spoke of, and I forgive you, too."

The leader took Jacinto's hand and stood to embrace him. Each of the others kissed and embraced Jacinto as a sign of their new fellowship.

The ghostly knights sheathed their swords and faded away.

Clear Water

Cantiga 321

Córdoba, Spain, 1265

Vela scooped her weakly moaning daughter out of bed and covered her with their faded cloak. She glanced up and down the lane to be sure no one would see them, wended through the whitewashed streets of their neighborhood, and reached the Roman bridge. At six years old, Toda was too big to carry, but her mother didn't know what else to do. The girl was too weak to walk to the cathedral.

In the middle of the bridge, Vela needed to rest. She collapsed onto the wide, smooth stones, because Toda couldn't have stood or sat on her own. Vela brushed the hair from her daughter's face, slick with sweat and teardrops. When Vela caught her breath and stood up again, the girl seemed even heavier than before.

"It's going to be all right, my love," her mother whispered into her hair, although she didn't believe it.

At this early hour, the people crossing the bridge were burdened with baskets or sacks full of market goods and hurried by without offering help. One man with a cart full of vegetables must've come from far away, because he didn't recognize Vela or her afflicted daughter. He halted his donkey and came close.

Vela didn't bother to speak. She shifted her daughter in her arms so the kind man could see the angry red lumps on her daughter's neck glisten in the slanted sunlight.

He backed away in horror. "Scrofula!"

Toda startled and cried out, then wept into her mother's tunic.

"You needn't explain, it's all right," Vela said as the man scrambled to drive his donkey away from the girl and her mother as fast as possible. "I know you can't have my plagued daughter in your cart with your fresh, healthy vegetables." She didn't have a free hand to wipe at her own tears.

"Mama, it hurts," Toda rasped.

"I know, sweet girl. We're going to get you all better."

The painful lumps had appeared on Toda's neck three years before. They started the size of a small coin under the right side of her jaw and had grown with her. Now, surrounded by dark bruising, they overtook her neck and pushed her earlobe upward. Her mother had watched her go from a curious toddler, always getting into things, to a miserable misshapen form, constantly weeping with pain. Toda probably didn't remember what it had been like to run about, to be interested in the world, to laugh.

That morning, Vela had woken to a terrifying rattle coming from under Toda's blanket. She couldn't catch her breath, but gawked at Vela as if Death itself had forced the door and watched from the corner. Vela knew this was her daughter's last chance.

They reached the customs tower at the end of the bridge and

fell into place in the queue. The cathedral loomed silently ahead of them, a solid fortress of faith.

"Not long now," Vela whispered into her daughter's ear. The line moved quickly; both the knights in charge of the bridge tax and the merchants lacked interest in delaying market trade.

There had been a time when Toda would've reached for the florid red cross embroidered on the knight's tunic. But now the knight had time to look them over calmly in the wide archway without having to deflect her daughter's inquisitive hands.

"I need to enter the cathedral to pray to Saints Cosmas and Damian for my daughter." Vela lifted her daughter's hair away from her neck.

The knight balked. "Is she bewitched?"

"She suffers from scrofula," said Vela. "So you see, I need to pray right now."

The knight backed against the wall and held his hand to his mouth. "Go ahead, but keep away."

"Do you know where Saints Cosmas and Damian have their altar?"

"It's next to the wall on the left, eight rows in." He waved his hands, shooing them through.

"Thank you," Vela choked. She had lived through worse brushoffs and shunning over the last three years, but feeling alone in the world with her worry never got easier. "Good day."

One step, then another, with Toda heavier every passing moment, Vela skirted the high walls of the golden-stone cathedral. It had been a mosque until King Fernando, the Saint, consecrated it for Christian worship, some thirty years before. The Moors who built the enormous structure had no pity for a poor Christian woman trying to heal her only daughter. They seemed to have kept adding stones until the building stretched into infinity. Vela had visited the cathedral many times before, but it had never taken her so long to reach the gate that led into the orange grove.

At last, she turned. The orange trees stood before her, leafy soldiers in orderly ranks. The green shade and whispering of the leaves made her pause. Maybe it really was going to be all right.

Vela crossed into the vast, echoing sacred space and waited a moment for her vision to adjust to the checkered light filtering through the jalousie windows and doorways. Slowly, the tables set up as temporary altars came into view between the marble columns. Ahead, the main altar drank in a stream of brilliance from the skylight. Even it wasn't much more than a cloth-covered table with candles and a portable altar the bishop opened before every mass and closed afterward. The other altars were regularly moved around the enormous grid of the cathedral, so Vela was glad she'd asked for the knight's indications. Other people seemed to be taking strolls to see where the saints of their devotion had been placed.

"One row, two rows—look, Toda, look at all the columns. It's like being in the forest, and the branches are red-and-white striped!"

The girl's eyes fluttered open and closed again. In one last effort, Vela hefted her daughter past three, four, five, six, seven, eight rows and stopped.

The table against the wall was covered with a simple linen cloth, probably a donation from someone who'd been cured. Two small wooden images of Saints Cosmas and Damian, the twin physicians, showed each other the flask and jar they carried, the tools of their trade. Their happy round faces and brightly colored robes struck hope into Vela's weary heart. Too many candles to count lined the edges and filled in the gaps between the images, though only a few were lit. Vela didn't have money to bring a candle. She hoped her prayers would burn bright enough for the saints to hear.

"See there, my darling? We've come to the right place. These doctors never charge for their services to good Christians."

She placed Toda before the altar and arranged her cloak so she wouldn't catch a chill on the cold stones. Vela knelt beside her daughter as if presenting an offering. She pressed her hands together and shut her eyes.

"Dear saintly doctors, I've come to ask you to restore the health of my daughter. Her name is Toda, because she means everything to me. Toda fell ill when she was only three years old, much too innocent to suffer so dreadfully. Over these three years, I've brought her before every doctor I could find. I've spent more than 50 *maravedíes*. That would be five years' income if my husband were still alive. It was all I'd had saved and all I earned in those years, and it would've been a small price for Toda's health. But for all their talk, poultices, and tisanes, none has been able to help at all. My daughter has only gotten worse, and now I also have debts I'll never be able to pay. I couldn't even keep enough scraps to make my daughter a doll. She never plays or laughs. St. Cosmas and St. Damian, you are the only physicians whose services I can afford. I have nowhere else to turn. Please, please, give my daughter back to me. I beg you humbly with all my heart, for it's all I have left to give."

She unclasped her hands to wipe at her tears before they fell on Toda. Vela rested her hand on her daughter's chest, which struggled to rise and fall. How long before she would know whether the prayers had worked? Surely no saint would let a little girl die in the cathedral. Would they? She would wait right there patiently because she had no other hope. She closed her eyes and breathed slowly and regularly, trying to show Toda how it was done.

She opened her eyes to wipe at them again and startled to see a man standing above her. The candles cast their golden light on the embroidery of his velvet surcoat, and when he bowed, the fat purse tied to his belt clinked with coins.

"Pardon me, lady. I'm Don Sandino, and you are?"

She sniffed and didn't dare stand up before him. "My name is Vela, and I'm praying for my daughter."

"Yes, I couldn't help but hear. Will you let me see what ails her?"

Vela moved the cloak away from Toda's neck. Don Sandino knelt and looked but kept his hands far from the girl as she twisted away.

"Is it scrofula?"

"Yes," Vela whispered.

"The saints are watching over you today, for they've sent me to find you and tell you that King Alfonso is in Córdoba this week, and I can take you to speak with him."

Vela looked into Don Sandino's eyes, trying to understand what the king had to do with her daughter.

"Don't you know?" he said, standing. "Scrofula is the king's evil. God has granted all Christian kings the ability to alleviate this pain with just a touch of their hand. In France and England, people suffering this disease assemble in great numbers. Their kings come to them and cure them instantly. King Louis in France has cured many young children like your daughter. King Alfonso must be holding audience this morning. I can take you to the castle right now. I'll tell him about your daughter, and I'm sure he'll have mercy and come to your aid."

"Just a touch of the hand?" Vela couldn't believe three years of suffering might end so quickly. "What do you think, darling? Do you want to go and see the king? This man says the king can make you all better."

"I'm cold," came the weak reply.

Vela lifted Toda. Don Sandino's sudden appearance just as she was praying had to be a sign. "Take us to the king."

Vela could hardly keep up with Don Sandino's long strides, even though it was all she wanted. When he darted through the gate out of the orange patio, she was afraid she would lose him in the crowds. "Don Sandino!"

The man turned back while the people in the street rushed around him.

She leaned on the archway. "I can't go so fast. She's heavy."

He arrived in the archway and regarded them. Vela instinctively covered Toda's face to protect her from scrutiny. She coughed, and any idea Don Sandino might've had about carrying her himself was gone. His hand corrected its course from her daughter to Vela's shoulder.

"I'll hold you up," he said. He cleared people and animals out of their path as they cut across the busy street and guided Vela with gentle pressure on her back.

The castle was made of the same golden stones as the cathedral. Though the cathedral dwarfed it, its Moorish towers were tall. They entered through the archway in a square tower, where the guard nodded at Don Sandino in recognition. Relief flooded through Vela. This potential savior was telling the truth.

They hurried along the wall through the courtyard, where people bustled about their daily tasks. Some men conversed under turbans or pointed caps, and some women clutched veils about their faces in the shade of the battlements. The tallest tower had many sides, making it even more imposing, and Vela thought it must be the homage tower. A guard at its gate nodded at Don Sandino, but observed Vela and Toda out of the corner of his eye.

"Is the king hearing pleas this morning?" asked Don Sandino. "I have a very special request on behalf of this lady's daughter."

Vela made sure the guard could see Toda's thin but sweet face. The girl blinked at him weakly and moaned.

"Yes, King Alfonso is in the assembly hall, but there could be a long wait. What is your request?"

Vela shifted Toda and the cloak fell open. The knight gasped and backed up. Vela wept in desperation.

"King Alfonso is this lady's best hope to save her daughter's life," said Don Sandino. "Don't you see? We have no time to wait."

The knight twisted his mouth and sighed. "Follow me."

He started up the staircase, which was just wide enough to let him hold his lance at his side. Don Sandino insisted Vela go first and patiently climbed the stairs behind her slow, heavy steps. She had long since lost sight of the guard when a well-dressed man came hurrying down and they had to stop against the wall for him to pass. Vela thought she would tumble down in his wake, too weak to continue upward, but Don Sandino on the step behind made sure she never lost her balance or her hold on Toda. At last, she rounded a corner and the knight was waiting in a doorway.

"I've spoken with the man who's next to speak with the king, mentioning your urgency," the guard told Don Sandino. He pointed though the doorway. "You're to sit in front of him, and you'll be next."

He headed back down, and Vela's eyes grew wide as she peered into the assembly hall. Light poured into the space from windows high in the vaulted ceiling and illuminated especially the far wall, where the king leaned on the arm of a chair on a raised platform. He was enveloped in a red velvet robe embroidered with castles and lions along the hem.

Although the tapestry behind the king with the same castles and lions dominated the room, Vela was relieved to see his lively eyes and patient expression. A man stood before him and made his case inaudibly. To the king's right, a boy of about ten wearing a castles-and-lions cap sat rigidly in a smaller chair, his gaze darting between the man and the king. He must be Fernando, the young heir. More guards in white tunics stood at attention along the wall.

Don Sandino huffed at Vela and stepped in front of her. He waded through the people seated on cushions throughout the rest of the hall and stooped to speak quietly with a man alarmingly near the thrones. After a handshake and nods, he waved to Vela. She stumbled along the same path Don Sandino had taken, whispering her apologies to the hands she stepped on and sides she stumbled over.

There was no time to sit down. The king told the man before him, "That's my final word. Please do not take up this plea again without more proof and documentation." The man bowed and headed for the doorway.

Don Sandino stepped into his place before the king. The man who was letting them go ahead told Vela, "Go on, don't be afraid."

But Vela was. She dared not look the king in the face. He seemed so high up there on his throne, there was no way he could possibly see her and her poor daughter. She sat Toda upright and knelt on the floor behind her, fidgeting endlessly.

Impossibly, the king nodded at Vela. "You needn't kneel before me. Stand up."

Vela's mouth opened, but no sound came out. Don Sandino bowed and said, "Your Majesty," drawing the king's gaze away from her.

"Good morning, Don Sandino. What brings you to our audience today?"

"I found this good lady in the cathedral. Forgive her if she doesn't rise. She is mightily weary from carrying her daughter all morning."

"Why must the girl be carried?"

"This lady, Vela by name, was praying to Saints Cosmas and Damian for a cure for her daughter. She's seen every physician in Córdoba over the last three years, and though she's spent a fortune on their cures and advice, not a single one has been able to help. When I saw the girl's neck, I knew to bring her to you right away. The girl suffers the king's evil. I knew that you, Your Majesty, in your great mercy, would be able to take away this child's suffering when so many physicians could not, and better than the King of France or—"

"Shut up, just be still. I can already give you my answer." The king shook his head. The red carbuncle on the front of his golden crown glinted in the sunlight. "You chatter like a stork, but what you say isn't worth a rotten fig. When you say I have miraculous powers, you make yourself a fool. I have no such powers. I am only a man who, by the grace of God, serves his subjects as king. Note this well, Fernando."

The boy at his right sat forward, nearly tipping out of his chair. The king addressed Vela directly, and for a moment, she couldn't hear what he said over her pounding heart.

"You would do well to leave earthly medicine and physicians alone. They can never help your daughter."

Three years of begging physicians for help and hiding at home because the neighbors spat and cursed at Toda. The terrifying morning of waking up to Toda's death rattle and doubting she had the power to carry Toda to their last prospect in the cathedral. Hope had risen in the form of Don Sandino only to be swept away at the top of a tower in the presence of a king who gave voice to Vela's worst fears. Toda was condemned to a desperate and painful death not even the worst sinner deserved, maybe before Vela could get her home.

A tear fell down Vela's cheek. When it hit Toda's cloak, it seemed to echo through the chamber.

The king appeared not to notice. "But fortune is with you. I know someone who can help you. Let us hear mass together."

The king stood, his robe falling gracefully around his form. He nodded at the prince, who took his father's place on the throne. King Alfonso crossed the room, the crowd easily parting before him, and Don Sandino fell in behind him.

Vela briefly wondered what the other people waiting would do, then hefted a bitterly whimpering Toda back into her arms. She didn't catch up with the men's swift steps until they waited for her at the homage tower gate. The guard winked at Vela, and she nearly dropped Toda in her surprise.

When her eyes had adjusted to the light, Vela noticed all the soldiers in the courtyard, polishing their steel and cleaning up the barracks. Neither the king nor Don Sandino were gawking, of course. The king received the soldiers' reverences with a friendly wave, but headed straight through the door in the tower opposite the one they'd just left.

"Thank God and all the saints," said Vela when, through the archway, she saw that the men weren't headed up the stairs. A large doorway to the side of the staircase opened into a chapel, where the priest listened to the king's instructions. Toda was speaking so weakly, her mother had to put her ear to the girl's mouth.

"Mama, I'm so tired. Can we go home?"

"We're going into a chapel now where you can rest," Vela said, but marched straight to Don Sandino. He stood near the altar and the king, and Vela whispered so the king wouldn't hear. "Did you ask the king what he intends to do?"

"It's the Blessed Mother of God," he said, beaming. "The king says Mary is the one who can help you."

Vela had expected another doctor, or even, in her wildest dreams, the king's personal physician. Why did these men think the Virgin could provide a cure where St. Cosmas and St. Damian couldn't?

"Dear lady," said the king, "please rest with your daughter on this bench. The priest is going to say a mass, and then I shall personally prepare the celestial medicine your daughter needs."

Dazed, Vela sat and helped Toda wrap her cloak around her for warmth. The girl's head drooped onto her mother's shoulder before the priest had returned from the sacristy. He knelt in front of the image of St. Mary, and Vela noticed her for the first time. The Blessed Virgin wore a delicate crown of gold wires with crystals that hung from the peaks and sparkled in the candlelight. Her eyes shone just as brightly, and with her half-smile, she seemed to regard the chapel as a good queen would regard her subjects, calm and patient. A voluminous purple velvet cloak studded with jewels covered most of her body, but her Son gazed out from the center of her lap, his hand raised in blessing.

As the priest intoned a gruff Salve Regina, Vela felt the blessing of the Virgin and Child flow over her and onto Toda, who slept peacefully. Vela dared not stand or kneel with the king and Don

Sandino for fear of disturbing her daughter's sleep. It might be the very thing that cured her after all that time, with celestial help.

Hardly any time passed before the mass was over and the priest stepped beside the altar, awaiting the king's instructions.

"Please remove Our Lady's cloak," the king told him. He hesitated, but the king turned to Don Sandino.

"Don Sandino, would you be so good as to get a bucket from the soldiers in the courtyard and fill it with clear water from the cistern?"

The nobleman also doubted for a moment, but made a slight bow and left the chapel. Vela couldn't help but wonder what the king had in mind. She watched the priest remove the Virgin's cloak and carefully fold it before carrying it to the sacristy. Aside from the colorful faces, the statue was unpainted wood and formless lumps that should've been arms, legs, and a chair. It was clearly not meant to be denuded in this way. Vela felt just as naked when she realized she and her daughter were alone with the king.

"Have no fear," he said. His voice was warm, and Vela wanted to believe that there was no reason to be afraid.

The priest came out to the altar. "I'm so sorry, Holy Queen," he told the image. "I know not what the king has planned, but I'm certain you'll be returned to your former dignity soon."

He looked askance at the king. Vela wondered at his daring. Didn't the king have ultimate authority, even here? King Alfonso might've said something, but Don Sandino returned with the bucket full of water.

"Very good," said the king. "Would you please set it here, in front of this good lady and her daughter?"

Vela felt her face burn with embarrassment. Toda jarred awake. "What's going on?" she rasped.

"I don't know, my dear." Vela and Toda watched wide-eyed as the king genuflected and made the sign of the cross, murmuring, then gingerly lifted the Virgin and Child from the altar and carried the image high as if in procession to Vela and Toda. He submerged it in the bucket slowly so the water wouldn't slosh out.

The priest's hands went to his head as if to contain his surprise, then he made the sign of the cross over and over again, but dared not say anything against the king's wishes.

Don Sandino hurried to help, holding his hand over the image so it wouldn't bob up while the king pushed back his sleeves.

King Alfonso glanced behind him. "Would you be so kind as to bring a linen?"

The priest darted into the sacristy and returned with an absorbent cloth. He stood beside the king helplessly as His Majesty massaged the clear water into the statue's nooks with his bare royal fingers. He caressed the eyes and lips of both faces with special care, then submerged the whole thing one last time and held out his hand for the linen.

Vela had felt certain the cleaning would carry off some of the image's paint, not to speak of what the water could do to the bare wood. But as the king dabbed at the image over the bucket, making sure no water was lost, it was obvious that the figure had come out brighter than before. The vermillion lips and golden swirls glowed, and Vela couldn't even look at the azure of their eyes. She couldn't help leaning forward to look into the bucket, and there were no traces of paint or splinters or even dust.

"There," the king said, satisfied. "You may put her cloak back on now." He handed the image to the priest, who fumbled a little before placing it meticulously back on the altar.

When the priest had returned to the sacristy for the cloak, the king lifted the communion cup from the altar. He brought it to the bucket, and looking Vela in the eye, said, "This is the chalice where humble wine from the vineyards becomes the blood of Christ, which saves us. Use it to let your daughter drink this pure water in which I've washed the image of the Blessed Virgin and Child."

Vela's throat was too dry to express her shock. The king put the chalice into her shaking hands. She dipped it in the bucket and brought it to her daughter's fevered lips.

"Drink, Toda. It's good. It will cure you."

Slowly, carefully, she tipped the cup toward Toda, who sipped listlessly, letting too much dribble down her chin.

"Like that, Your Majesty?" Vela asked without looking at the king's face.

"Very well," he replied above her. "Leave the bucket full of this water here, and come every day to let your daughter drink for as many days as there are in Mary's name when it's written down in Latin."

Vela looked at Don Sandino's waving hand behind the king. He held up all five digits. "Five, so if this is the first, we come for four more days."

"Exactly," said King Alfonso. "On the fifth day, her suffering will be finished, and the girl will be well."

Vela was overwhelmed with gratitude. She grasped the royal hands and kissed each one of the eight rings on them.

"Save your thanks for the Mother of God when your daughter is well." He gently pulled his hands away. "Don Sandino, they shouldn't have to travel to come here every day. Show them to the guest quarters off the garden. The girl will enjoy the plants and the ponds when she feels better."

Don Sandino and Vela bowed, and the king swept out of the

chapel. Vela waited while Don Sandino explained to the priest what would happen over the next few days. She arranged Toda's cloak and caressed her face. Did she feel a bit less warm? The girl felt less burdensome as Vela followed Don Sandino through the courtyard to the gardens.

"Look, Toda. So many different trees! And listen to the fountains." The sounds of the river they heard ceaselessly in their home had never been so comforting. Toda sighed. Did she sound less in pain?

Don Sandino opened the door of a room built against the wall that enclosed the castle gardens. Light poured in through a window onto a large bed and a table with a mirror, a basin, and a couple of books on top. There was plenty of room under the table for a trunk full of clothes, but Vela had no such luggage. These must be the quarters of traveling dignitaries.

"I hope you'll be comfortable here while your daughter gets well," said Don Sandino.

"You mean this isn't your room?" said Vela. "We stay here, in the palace?" She set Toda on the bed and the girl sat staring at the rich surroundings.

"We'll have meals brought to you here, so you needn't worry about anything." He considered Toda's fixed gaze. "And I'll see if we can find a toy. She'll need one, or a few, soon."

Vela knelt and kissed his hands. "I don't know what I've done to deserve such treatment after so many years of being shunned. Is there any work I could do to repay you and the king? I can sew and mend, card and weave, make thread… I could shear sheep, but I'm sure they've already been this year."

"There's no need. Take care of your daughter." He closed the door as he left.

Vela went to the window and watched him stride back to the

castle. When she turned around, Toda was wiggling her legs and looked like she would fall off the bed.

Vela caught her in her arms. "What do you want, my love?"

"Window!" said Toda. Her mother carried her one last stretch and set her on the cushioned bench so she could look out at the gardens. Her breathing seemed more normal than it had been for days if not weeks. When Vela put her hand to Toda's forehead, it seemed warm, but not burning hot. Vela let herself get lost in imaginary walks through the gardens.

When they saw the royal page coming with a large tray, Vela realized she was too hungry to speak. She opened the door for the servant, who greeted them and placed the tray in her hands, removing the wooden cover with a flourish.

There were two ceramic plates overflowing with meat, fish, rice, and vegetables, and huge hunks of white bread at the side as well as a jar full of wine. There were also three little bowls with different colorful sauces and another bowl with rose petals floating on the surface. The page left before she could ask him what it was for, but she soon figured out that it was for rinsing their hands between courses.

Vela took the tray to the bed. "What would you like to eat? We have our choice here," she told her daughter.

"I'm not hungry." Her head drooped.

Vela laid her out on the side of the bed without the tray, and she fell asleep. Vela set out to clean her plate. She wasn't sure which sauce to use with what dish, so she tried them all with everything. The rich flavors piled up on each other, urging her to add more to her palate. She paused and looked at her weary daughter before wiping the ceramic with the bread and devouring it, too.

The other plate was meant for Toda. Vela still felt a vast

emptiness in her stomach. There was no way her daughter would eat all this food. She finished the sauces, meat, fish, and vegetables, but left some rice and bread, just in case. Finally sated, she left the tray by the door and climbed in with her daughter to sleep.

The morning light was crystalline, but Vela woke to Toda's rasping. She felt her daughter's forehead, and it was cool, free of fever for the first time in three years. Vela wept a tear of joy. Then there was a knock at the door.

She stepped over the tray and opened it to a hearty woman. She held a doll sewn out of linen, dressed in a red velvet gown, with hair made from golden silk strands tied up under a white linen cap. The doll could've been a queen's maid or a lady with a great estate, so much better than any rag doll she might've made with the scraps of wool she'd had to sell to pay the doctors.

"Good morning. I'm here to help you get your daughter to the chapel for mass. And I have this gift for her." She held out the doll, and Vela took it reluctantly, hardly daring to touch something so fine.

"It's so beautiful," she said. "Where did it come from?"

"The queen heard about you and your daughter yesterday, and in the afternoon, between all of her ladies, we found scraps and made it."

"Thank you so much. What wonderful scraps the queen has!" She took the doll to the bed. "Toda, darling, it's time to wake up. And look what the queen and her ladies made for you."

Still rasping, the girl opened her eyes. She made a sound between a cough and gasp of delight and brought the doll to her heart.

"It's time to go to the chapel," said the woman. She leaned over

Toda and took her in her arms, doll and all. Vela's former friends had recoiled and accused Toda of being touched by the Devil. The woman's simple tenderness had become extraordinary to Vela.

"She has no fever today. I think the Blessed Virgin's medicine is already working!" Vela babbled as they returned to the castle through the gardens. She felt none of the exhaustion of the day before.

Along with many other people of the king's court, Don Sandino was in the chapel to make sure the priest followed the king's instructions. He sat on the bench on the other side of Toda, but they found that they were able to stand and kneel as the mass progressed. Vela looked into the eyes of the image and prayed her gratitude for relieving the fever. Toda sat patiently, quietly rasping and clasping the doll, and coughing once in a while, but she was never at risk of falling off the bench.

When the priest had wiped the chalice and was folding the linen, Don Sandino brought the bucket from beside the altar. He looked sternly at the priest, who lifted the chalice with both hands and presented it to Vela.

"The cure might be even stronger if you give it to my daughter," said Vela. "I'm only her mother, but you're God's intermediary."

"Very well," the priest huffed, but his face relaxed. He dipped the chalice in the water with utmost care and brought it to Toda's lips. She coughed, and he retreated but tried again right away. This time, Toda accepted the water, only dribbling a little onto her doll's cap.

Later, when they brought the tray to the room, Toda ate some of the meat, rice, and bread. In the afternoon, she held her doll on the bench by the window and looked at the pictures Vela pointed out in the books from the table. They agreed the Virgin Mary in the pictures looked a lot like her doll. When Vela saw bizarre monsters, she flipped the page. When the girl felt sleepy, Vela noticed her breathing was gentle, with no difficulty, exactly the way a sleepy six-year-old ought to breathe.

She felt so happy and grateful, she hardly slept before the sun peeked through the window to reveal Toda making the doll dance an elaborate jig, singing softly. "Hi, Mama," she said as if every day started that way.

Vela counted. It was day three, and already her daughter was a different child. Vela felt overwhelmed imagining how their lives would be different on the fifth day. She nearly fell over, getting the door when the maid appeared.

Don Sandino wasn't in the chapel that morning, but after Toda drank from the priest's hand, Vela leaned in to kiss her, and could hardly see the subtle redness on Toda's neck. The lumps still pushed her earlobe upward, but most of the irritation was a bad memory.

That day, in the room, Toda smiled and ate, ate and smiled, until she finished her plate. Vela let her have all the sauce she wanted. She was too busy playing with her doll to be bothered with the pictures in the books. "Fountain," she said. "Can we go to the fountain?"

The sun was low. "All right, but just for a few minutes," said Vela.

She carried Toda to the burbling fountain they could see from the window, had her sitting comfortably, and held the doll out of harm's way. Toda put her hand in the water's flow to spray everything around and laugh with abandon. Vela hardly recognized her daughter's voice, disguised as it was in childlike joy.

On the morning of the fourth day, Vela woke to Toda's tugging at the covers from her place beside her. "Why are you so sleepy, Mama?" she said. "It's time to visit St. Mary."

She was right. The queen's maid knocked at the door. Vela hurried to prepare herself while the maid ran a comb through Toda's hair. When she looked up, the maid had pulled back Toda's hair into two braids. The morning sun reflected off her neck as off a mirror because the skin was free of redness and perfectly smooth. Her little earlobe hung down, free of the welts' pressure.

"What a pretty girl," said the queen's maid, and took her into her arms to carry her.

Vela fetched the doll from the bed and followed behind them. She handed the doll to her daughter, who smiled and laughed. Vela couldn't help grinning, too.

"I can hardly believe how well she is. It's only the fourth day, and we haven't given her any hot baths or medicinal syrups aside from the water in the bucket."

"Someone who might be cured after many years of medical treatment, or never recover at all, can always be made whole again by St. Mary," said the maid. "Everyone at court knows St. Mary's power is greater than any medicine."

Vela concentrated on the regal image on the altar, trying to read her placid half-smile. She couldn't help thinking about what was under the voluminous purple cape. Take it away, and Mary and her Child were as simple as Vela and Toda. How was it possible that this wooden queen was working such wonders in her daughter?

Unexpected movement at her side pulled her out of her thoughts. Toda was standing, all on her own. She was a perfect imitation of the adults, smoothly kneeling, and even making sure the doll showed due respect, as well. Vela folded her hands and thanked St. Mary and her Son, even though it was not a time to speak during the mass. Other members of court could be heard behind them, murmuring and gasping as they realized that this was the same girl who had been a lump of suffering only days before.

When the priest brought the chalice, Toda rose to meet it. She drank down the clear water and wiped her mouth with her sleeve. The queen's maid moved to take her, but Vela held out her hand to stop her.

"Toda, can you walk back to our room? Maybe if I hold your hand?"

"All right, Mama," said the girl, taking her hand and falling into step, the doll in her other arm. They marched through the arms patio of the castle with all the soldiers stopping to gawk at them, and Toda started to skip and pull at her mother to go faster.

They left the castle. The sun glinted on the pools and a light breeze played in the leaves of the trees. Toda looked up at her mother with a mischievous glint in her eye. She let go of her mother's hand. Before Vela knew what was happening, Toda broke into a run and was lost in the garden, only her laughter giving her away.

Vela fell to her knees on the turf and wept with gratitude to the Lady who gives life to those who love her Son.

ꬍaded Threads

Cantiga 341

Le-Puy-en-Velay, France,
thirteenth century

I like to climb the 268 steps to St. Michel's chapel, alone on its rock pinnacle, as often as I can because St. Michel should be honored. But also, from up here, the valley opens out beneath me as if I were a bird. The leaves on the trees and shrubs far below dance whether they're yellow with springtime or ochre with autumn. The mountains swell around the river like the backs of dragons, majestic even in their sleep. God's artistry is nowhere more obvious than here.

When the wind whips my threadbare skirts around my legs, and I have to press my cap to my head so it won't fly away, I'm reminded that I mustn't let the beauty overtake me, or I might topple over the ledge and end up in pieces on the roofs below.

My father climbed up here every day. He led me up as many steps as my little legs could manage and then carried me to kneel beside him in the chapel and whisper prayers for my mother. I'm lucky my father cared for me as well as he did after my mother died. I'm even luckier that Raoul married me before my father died because this way, I was never an orphan. Never just an orphan. Now I'm a wife first. The tailor's wife, no less. And maybe, somehow, someday, I'll be a mother, too.

Before we were married, Raoul joined me on my walks up to St. Michel, lit candles, and recited prayers with me. He told me he would make me dresses that were even finer than the cloaks of the Blessed Virgin. When we had our first child, he said, he would drape the entire chapel with cloth of gold for the baptism. I only laughed, knowing they couldn't do that even for the baptism of a prince.

Raoul is away at the market in Saint-Etienne. It's the first time he's been away so long, and I think I'll be lonely. As I make my way down the steps, I decide to ask Amée and Isabeau to help me sort and card the wool he left for me this morning. I have to avoid coming down too hard on my left ankle or it will give out under me. I must've tripped on the steps coming up. That's what I'll tell my friends.

Amée and Isabeau live with their parents—the miller and his wife—near the Cathedral of Our Lady of Le Puy, so I stop at the altar and say a prayer for the quick healing of my ankle. In the presence of the Blessed Virgin, Mother of us all, I feel so protected and at peace, it's almost as if I'm not an orphan.

When I rap on the door of their house, Amée answers and invites me in. Their open windows and cooking fire fill me with welcoming warmth, but I remain at the threshold.

"I have a lot of wool to prepare for cloth. Could you and Isabeau help me today?"

The young ladies embrace their mother, tell her *au revoir*, and accompany me chatting and laughing down the street. My ankle is twinging now and swelling so that the laces of my boots dig into my flesh, but I don't make a sound. I pay attention to my friends instead of the discomfort.

"Cateline, shouldn't the tailor use fabrics others have already made?" asks Amée.

"That's where Raoul is now," I explain. "Buying fabric in Saint-Etienne. But he said the mayor gave him wool to make the cape with, so we must use what he gave us. We can make better fabric than my husband can buy anywhere, right, girls?" Cheered by their presence, I smile and greet everyone we see along the way.

When we open the door to the shop, I see I've left it a mess. The windows are shut and the wool is a grey shadow that trails from the work table to the back room, where I know it's all over the bedstead. Amée and Isabeau stare at me and then at each other. I'm dismayed I've chosen this moment to invite them over after more than a year since the wedding. They must be shocked, but they say nothing.

Isabeau opens the windows and lights a fire while Amée helps me gather the wool into a manageable heap on the work table. Mice skitter into the walls with stolen bits of fluff as we move their briefly adopted home. Soon we're settled on the benches, making piles with carders at the ready.

"The cloak is going to be black with blue and gold embroidery," I explain. "I think there's plenty here to make both the cloth and the embroidery thread. I'm not sure if we'll get any gold thread, so maybe we should set aside some of this mess to dye yellow, just in case." I always find a way to salvage a situation in case something goes wrong.

"You work very hard," says Amée. "Raoul won't even need an apprentice with you here. He must kiss your feet every night."

My ankle twinges at the thought and my leg jumps. Isabeau's gaze darts toward the movement, and I realize faded threads have come loose at the bottom of my skirt and are snagging the top of my boot's toe, which has split open.

Isabeau speaks as if to no one in particular. "I would think the tailor's wife would be the best-dressed lady in town."

"This is my best dress," I say before I can stop myself. Amée and Isabeau know it: in the absence of my mother, they placed the garlands on my head at my wedding. That day, I first wore the dress, all green and velvety, and felt like a queen walking up to the church door. I wore out my work dress in the first year, then my second-best dress fell into rags, but Raoul always has a purpose for the fabric he brings to the shop. I've been mending my wedding dress with leftover scraps too useless to put in the poor box at the cathedral.

Amée and Isabeau card the wool in silence. I concentrate so hard, I'm startled when Amée sneezes and coughs.

"The fuzz is drying my throat, too," says Isabeau. "Have you anything to drink?"

My body goes too cold for my weak heart to warm it back up. "No."

"Nothing?" says Amée.

"At all?" says her sister, dropping her work.

"There are nine wineskins in the trunk," I begin, gesturing. I don't need to tell them Raoul has taken the key with him to Saint-Etienne. They can see the lock.

"What are you going to drink today, and until your husband comes home?" asks Isabeau.

"I was going to fill a bucket at the stream. It's clean, isn't it?"

"Water? From the stream? The tailor can afford for his wife to drink wine or at least ale, can't he?"

"What about food? What are you going to eat until Raoul returns?" says Amée.

I have no answer.

"Is Raoul hoping you'll die while he's gone? That's what it looks like."

"What have you done to deserve this treatment?" asks Isabeau.

I don't reply because I honestly don't know, and because sorrow stops my throat. This morning, before he left for Saint-Etienne, Raoul received the loose wool from the mayor's messenger. I awoke suffocating under something heavy and shapeless and my husband's voice muffled behind it but shouting as if he didn't care who heard.

"Do some good around here while I'm gone. Earn your keep! Get this wool ready for the mayor's cloak, and don't waste any. I can't afford to feed you and pay the dyer!"

I flailed in the cloudy fibers, and he reached through to hold my arms at my sides. I inhaled a ball of fluff and choked while Raoul wrenched my left ankle and pulled me out onto the floor. By the time I caught my breath and cleared the rest of the wool off my shift and out of my hair, my husband was gone.

My ankle is sending pain in red-hot wheels up my leg now.

Raoul chose me because he loved me. My friends saw it all. He didn't have to save me from an orphan's fate after my mother died, but he wanted me. He brought gifts of silk ribbons in every color to my father's house and never ceased telling me how beautiful I looked in them. The ribbons are gone now, and perhaps my beauty is, too, both used up mending my hopeless dresses. Could that be why he no longer loves me? Can any amount of work bring him back to me?

"I'm just an orphan. I'm lucky Raoul accepted me."

"Neither of us is married." Amée has come to put her arms around me.

Isabeau looks for something to wipe my tears. "Papa's apprentice is going to ask for me any day now," she says.

"But our father would never allow our husbands to treat us like this," Amée finishes. "There must be something we can do to help you."

"We're the miller's daughters," says Isabeau. "We can save some grain apart for you, and take it to the oven and bring you some bread."

"Don't be silly," her sister says. "Cateline, we'll take you to live with us and give you all the bread you can eat and wine you can drink."

My resistance fades as I become dizzy with the pain, and I'm considering going with them. But given how he's treating me without provocation, I think he might track me down and kill me if I appear to abandon him. "I can't leave here. Raoul will come back and find me gone."

"Let him," says Isabeau, hoisting me off the bench. She gets under my arm to support me on my faltering ankle, which surprises me a little since I haven't mentioned the pain at all. Amée stirs cold dirt into the fire so it will die, and we head out as if there was never any wool to work on.

Their house smells incredible with a pottage bubbling at the hearth. Isabeau sits me on a bench and tells me to stir the pot if it's about to boil over. I'm useful in spite of my leg, which she props up on the bench, too. It feels better already with the kindness, but my boot looks as if it will burst.

Amée has been whispering with their mother, who looks at me with a frown. When she comes near me, my heart is pounding. Will she throw me back into the street?

She reaches for my ankle. I flinch.

"Oh, you poor thing," she says, bending to hold me in her motherly arms. "You have no one in the world to protect you."

Already tears escape my eyes, and when she straightens up and says, "Of course you may stay here as long as you need to," I weep uncontrollably.

I can't hear or see anything until the spoon I'm holding clatters to the hearth. Amée rescues it with a practiced hand, and her mother sits next to my ankle as if nothing has happened. Delicately, she unties my boot lace, and I dry my tears and look at her dress. The miller must have money to spare. None of their clothes have been mended at all, but are bright and new.

"You seem like a good woman." Their mother pulls the boot lace out. "Why does he treat you this way?"

"I don't know." The sobs course through me again. Amée grabs me under the armpits and her mother pries the boot off my swollen foot. I hardly feel it. Amée lets go and between their gasps for air, I say, "There must be some reason. What could it be?"

The question haunts me for the next three days, in spite of the food and wine, the soft bed I share with the sisters, and the loving care my ankle receives. I remember the way Raoul used to protest when I helped around the workshop. "Leave that for the apprentices," he would say. "You're my wife." I would blush with pride. If I had injured my ankle two months ago, he might have let me sit by the hearth and brought me teas and poultices, the way Amée and Isabeau do now. But something must've happened two months ago, because since then, having a husband has been worse than being an orphan.

On the second day, the miller comes home with a cloth he's passed under the cloak of Our Lady of Le Puy. He places it on my ankle, and it feels cool and comforting. We pray Ave Maria five times, and when we're finished, I dare to rotate my foot. I can almost do it without pain, and the next morning, there's no more swelling. The miller, his wife, and their daughters join hands and dance around the bed while I keep time clapping.

I'm sitting at the hearth again with Isabeau, my leg much shapelier but still weak, when Amée bursts through the door, her face white.

"Word is running around town. The tailor wants to know where his wife is."

I take a deep breath and stand on both legs without help. "Good. I have a question for him, too."

I wobble and catch myself on the bench. Amée and Isabeau run to my aid, but I'm already standing up as tall as I can while keeping balance.

"Are you sure you want to see him now?" asks Isabeau.

"Why don't you rest for a few more days? Let him find you?" says Amée.

"No, I need to talk to him now and ask him my question," I say. "If you'll help me get there."

Amée, Isabeau, and their mother surround me as we make our way through the streets. Keeping up with their pace, sometimes hopping on my strong leg, distracts me from the rage I'm sure awaits me. I just have time to say Ave Maria and ask the Virgin Mother to protect me as I go before my husband's judgment.

The girls let me open the door, and I lean on the jamb. Inside, it looks worse than I left it. I don't remember scattering the loose wool on the floor and the hearth after Amée, Isabeau, and I so carefully gathered it up, but there it is. The mystery is solved when Raoul lunges out of the bedroom door, covered in fuzz. When he sees us, he stops short, but quickly gathers his thoughts.

"Where have you been? Why haven't you prepared this wool for the mayor?"

My legs are wooden posts because of the fear I feel before the look in his eyes. What happened to his love? How did I lose it? How can I get it back? I can't survive with a husband who hates me. It would almost be better to be alone in the world.

Amée grabs my hand and tosses her head back. "Cateline has a question for you, too," she says to Raoul.

"Oh? What would that be?" He raises his fists, responding to an unknown challenge.

I take a deep breath and cross myself, trusting the Mother of God. As long as Raoul stays across the room, I can do this. "Husband, I would like to know if you think people who have committed no crime should be punished."

He drops his fists and cocks his head. "Why do you ask?"

"Because I see that you are very angry with me, and it frightens me. I desire nothing so much as to know why." I blink to hold in the tears.

He crosses to me and reaches for my hands, but I don't let him take them. "I've been told by trustworthy men that you do me great wrong."

"What men were these?" asks Isabeau. "Who did they say she wronged you with? When did they tell you these lies?"

My husband ignores her. "I'd rather be dead than have a wife like that. I can never forgive such a thing. May ill fortune befall all who dishonor their husbands!"

"I'm not one of those women."

"May God give you the strength to endure such a false accusation," says Amée.

I nod, taking comfort in the way she, her sister, and their mother stand between me and Raoul. "I've never wronged you, nor would I ever. I'll do anything to prove my innocence." I think of all the possible trials by ordeal. I choose the one that seems most like the punishment Raoul has already put me through. "I'll walk through fire for all to witness."

My husband throws his hands up in surprise. "For God's sake, don't burn yourself in a fire."

"But I wouldn't burn," I insist, "because I'm not one of those women."

"No, no. If you must do something, I would have you go before the altar of Our Lady of Le Puy and swear for all to hear that you are innocent of these accusations I've heard, and that you've never done me wrong."

"Gladly. Let's go now." I turn, eager for this nightmare to end so easily.

"And then I want you to climb the pinnacle of St. Michel and leap from the top to join the other sinners."

My heart stops. It beats again only when Isabeau cries, "No!"

Half dreaming, I've seen myself fly from that pinnacle as if I were a bird almost every day of my life. But I've also seen what happens when people are pushed from the top of St. Michel in reality. It's the punishment for the most felonious criminals to die terrified and without sacraments.

"St. Mary, save me," I say. I look Raoul in the eye. "I'll do that, gladly, if afterward, you'll never have suspicions about me again."

His eyes wide, Raoul nods. "So be it."

I stride in the direction of the cathedral, my ankle as steady now as it ever was.

"You won't really do it, will you? You'll swear before the altar, and then he'll be satisfied," Amée says.

I look back at my husband, following us women. He's scowling. He never used to look on me with anything but a smile. He used to wake me with a gentle kiss and a cup of spiced wine. I would do anything to make him treat me like that again.

I don't answer Amée, but push open the cathedral door. They're singing Vespers mass, so the five of us stand in the back and sing the responses with everyone else. When it's over, I push through the crowd and place my hand on the altar at the feet of Our Lady.

"Virgin Mother, save me from false accusations. I swear by the Christian faith that I have never done my husband wrong, nor will I ever. I have only ever honored him and been as faithful as you were to Joseph, loving and fearing only God more than he. Queen of Heaven, protect me as I prove my innocence."

None of the people in the nave for mass have left when I turn around. There must be a hundred of them, probably including the men who besmirched my name. All of them and the miller join Amée, Isabeau, their mother, and my husband, following me as I parade through the town center just like prisoners must before they're pushed to their condemnation from the pinnacle. Some of them sing and attract even more people, so many that it seems it's time for the town festival.

The 268 steps have never required less effort. I feel almost weightless on my ankle. I reach the top under a cloudless sky before the others and must wait for them at the edge, where I normally feel so free. I look at the sky, hoping to glimpse the Virgin Mother and her Son, because I know they're watching, but then my eyes are drawn downward.

Someone even less lucky than the prisoners is tasked with clearing away the bodies below. Sometimes when I come to this summit, I see that they've missed pieces in the bushes or atop someone's roof tiles. I wonder if the prisoner is more tortured in the life to come without his foot. Or perhaps he's better off because there's less flesh to torture. I swallow, but my throat is dry with the fear of every criminal who has fallen this way before me. In this place set aside for harsh judgment, I have to remind myself that I'm no sinner.

When everyone has arrived, the pinnacle is so full, it wouldn't surprise me if some people fell off in the crowding. Raoul is standing with my friends. I wonder if he'll believe me, even if I survive. I can only be sure God and His Mother are with me.

"Help me convince this doubter, Holy Mother of God. Help me now, since you always help those who do no wrong."

Amée and Isabeau push through the crowd toward me, but townsmen hold them back. I throw off my dress and let it fall below.

I stand in my undergarment so I'm just like the leaping prisoners. I want everyone to see me as my husband does—as the criminal I'm not. My shift's fabric was thin to begin with, and now it's so worn, there's not a single person who can't see absolutely everything. They gasp and stare. But even with gooseflesh, I'm proud to stand before their judgment. On me they will find no stain, only faith that the Virgin Mother watches over me as her orphaned child, no matter how many pieces I'm in.

And I'm falling.

I've left the people far behind on the pinnacle.

It should frighten me. But it's as if I can feel the loving gaze of Mary and her Son pressing my shift to my skin and caressing my face, and it's smooth like a velvet cape. Or perhaps a mother's arms.

I hit bottom away from the buildings, and the shrubs feel soft, like the clouds in the painting behind the screen at the altar. What look like thorns and thick branches are more pliant than the wool that choked me before I invited my friends to card it.

I stand up. I expect to find that my body will stay behind, that my feet will be atop that roof, my hands under that bush, my skull broken upon those rocks. But I inspect my hands and test my feet, and they are definitely attached to my body. My ankle even twinges a little.

I've been carried to the ground with as much care as a mother lays her infant in a cradle, as if by the hand of Our Lady herself. Even if I'm alone in the world, I have the most important person watching over me from Heaven.

"Praise be to God and his Mother!" I shout as soon as I return to reason.

Raoul comes running around the base of the pinnacle to meet me, with all the other people behind him. Amée fishes my dress out of a nearby shrub and helps me pull it over my head so I'm not so cold. Raoul leads everyone in kneeling before me. He kisses my hands and sheds cleansing tears on them.

"Oh, Cateline, my darling wife, patient woman, saintly lady! Forgive me and my doubt in you, just as God pardons those who do wrong."

I smile at him, but don't have to decide what to say because I'm swept up onto the shoulders of people from the crowd. They parade me back through town in a reversal of the walk of the condemned.

I look back at Raoul, keeping up with the crowd. "That's my wife," he says to anyone and everyone. He waves at me and I recognize the husband I once knew.

I thank the Virgin Mary for bringing my benevolent protector back to me. I hope Raoul will agree to lay offerings of money and candles at the Virgin's altar for many years to come. Perhaps we'll go on pilgrimages to other sites where St. Mary has performed miracles.

They bring me inside the cathedral and set me before the altar. Everyone lines up to touch my head or kiss my hand.

The miller explains what happened to one of the priests, saying, "It's a miracle! Someone needs to write it down."

Historical Notes

The *Cantigas* are wonderful poetry, full of virtuosic linguistic devices and playful effects, because they were written by the best poets of the time. However, even the longest *cantigas* present skeletal narratives. Medieval narrators seem to have relied on their audiences to keep references to other literature and current events in mind and supply their own empathy while they listened. Because this assumed audience support has largely disappeared over time, a story that was emotionally effective in the Middle Ages can seem flat and lifeless to modern readers.

In fleshing out the narratives for this collection, I added almost everything a reader expects today: setting, scenes, characters, emotional depth, and the details that make the reader feel they're there with the characters. I translated and adapted dialogue when it appeared in the poems. Otherwise, the originals served principally as plot outlines.

In each note, I provide my literal translation of the refrain based on the Mettmann edition. These repeated lines point to the themes and even the morals of each story.

Figure 2: *Cantiga* 42. Escorial manuscript T.I.1.

My Glorious Bride:
Cantiga 42

The Most Glorious Virgin,
Spiritual Queen,
is jealous of those she loves,
since she doesn't want them to do wrong.

This legend may have originated in Roman times. While the *Cantigas* poet and the miniaturists take great care to explain why the image of St. Mary is outdoors, it would've been perfectly natural for an Ancient Roman to find a statue of Venus, for example, while out with friends. The motif became popular and made it into many European folklore traditions. The *Cantigas* collectors could've based their poem on any of seven known versions in English and French Latin-language miracle collections of the twelfth and thirteenth centuries, or on other versions that have since become lost.

The *cantiga* places this miracle in "Germany." I have little working knowledge of medieval Germany, which I think was also the case for at least a few of the *Cantigas* artists, because in the final panel (Figure 2), the pine trees, evoking a specific detail in the poem, look like rounded Iberian pine trees rather than the isosceles shape of pines of medieval Germany and the rest of the world. I therefore take the liberty of setting this story in an imagined Germany.

The song refers to the game the young men play as simply "pelota" (ball) (l. 19), going on to specify that it's the game young men most like to play (l. 20). The artists of the *Códice rico* manuscript were more explicit, designing a second panel that provoked American scholars to use the term "baseball" in the twentieth century (Keller and Cash; Keller and Kincade), complete with a pitcher, a batter, and outfielders (Figure 2). After seeing the miniature, there was no going back to simply "ball," but I knew using the word "baseball" would jar readers, and settled on calling it "stickball."

Panel 5 inspired the way the Virgin painfully twists Waltram's hand during her scandalous second appearance between him and his bride in their marriage bed. With this *cantiga*, my collection starts off by showing readers that St. Mary means business! I fleshed out the imagery in the dream visions to give Waltram specific "anguish" and add to his mortal dread a desire to protect the woman he's just married.

The original audience at Alfonso X's court would've considered this a happy ending because the faithful must keep their promises. If St. Mary permitted anyone to default on a promise to her, society would quickly devolve into chaos.

The Unwary Host:
Cantiga 67

*The Glorious Queen is of such great holiness,
that with it she defends us from the Devil and his evil.*

This miracle's potential sources include three extant French and one English manuscript from the twelfth and thirteenth centuries. The popularity of the tale probably contributes to its geographical vagueness: the *cantiga* text doesn't mention where this miracle takes place. I decided to set the story along the pilgrim's way to Santiago, which was a wildly popular route in the thirteenth century, because the plot called for a rich man to undertake many charitable projects. A pilgrims' hostel seemed the perfect recipient of Don Filadelfo's time and resources and the topic of his diary. I've visited Carrión de los Condes in the province of Palencia and marveled at its Romanesque architecture. It would've been natural for the bishop to make an appearance in such an important town from time to time.

The zombie element of the plot seemed attractive to readers across the centuries, and I'm afraid I made the reveal gorier than the *Cantigas* artists did (Figure 3). Their desiccated corpse in the sixth panel with the skeleton clearly outlined was probably enough to frighten anyone. I'm only sorry I couldn't figure out how to get around Don Filadelfo's blindness to the Devil's intentions so I could use a clever shorthand like the artists did, showing the demonic face on the back of Cresconio's head in panels 3, 4, and 5.

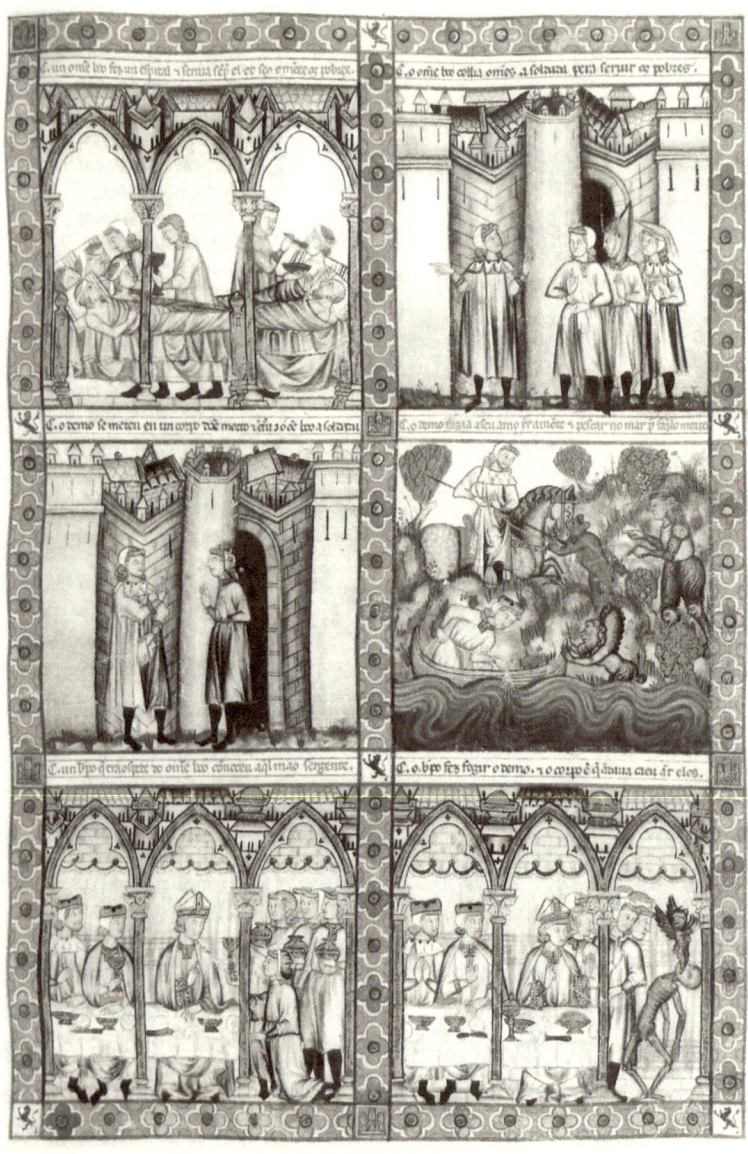

Figure 3: *Cantiga* 67. Escorial manuscript T.I.1.

182

The Lamb and the Wolf:
Cantiga 147

The Mother of Him who made Balaam's beast speak
later also made a sheep speak once.

The only possible source text that has survived for this *cantiga* is Rivipullensis 193 from the turn of the twelfth to the thirteenth century. Ripoll, which gives the manuscript its reference signature, is a lovely historic town at the foot of the Pyrenees in modern Catalunya. This region would've had intense cultural contact with southern France, so it makes sense that the monks at Ripoll would receive news from Rocamadour, where this miracle is set.

With this story, I wanted to highlight the role of animals in medieval life. Though they're utilized for commerce, animals have a way of endearing themselves to people, today and in the past. I based my character's affection for her special sheep on the beautiful animals with luxurious wool in the miniatures of *Cantiga* 147 (Figure 4), and decided that the miracle's protagonist should be a Spanish Merino. The illustrations also show the old lady cheerfully shearing her recovered sheep and taking the wool to St. Mary's shrine. My character begrudges giving up the miraculous wool a bit more, but her donation is necessary to maintain the Alfonsine sense of everything right with the world.

The music of this *cantiga* delightfully imitates the baaing of sheep, frequently dividing syllables near the ends of phrases into three or more separate descending notes (Casson, http://

Figure 4: *Cantiga* 147. Escorial manuscript T.I.1.

cantigasdesantamaria.com/csm/147#music/). The poem quotes the sheep's words: "Ey-m' acá" (Here I am) (l. 37). The musical phrasing invokes a sound that doesn't stretch the imagination and makes the miracle that much more believable.

The Castle Across the Stream: *Cantiga* 185

St. Mary has great power to help her own,
in whatever place they may be, and defend them
from evil.

An incident related to this miracle took place on the border of Castile with the Kingdom of Granada, probably at the beginning of the *mudéjar* uprising in 1264 (O'Callaghan, *Alfonso X* 112). The poet claims to have heard the miracle (rather than having read about it) from trustworthy witnesses, so the *cantiga* is the first time this incident has been recorded, and its very immediacy may imply partiality (Montoya, *Historia* 11). In other words, it hits close to home. This *cantiga's* importance as something Spanish listeners could identify with made it apt for placement at a number ending with 5. Such miracles received special treatment in the Alfonsine workshop, with longer text and two full pages of illustrations in the *Códice rico* instead of one.

The castellan (noble caretaker) of Chincoya Castle in 1264 was a man named Sancho Martínez de Jódar (O'Callaghan, *Alfonso X* 113), and this figure has a fictional counterpart in "The Castle Across the Stream." During his reasoning for trusting the castellan of Bélmez, he refers to the initial conquest of the Iberian Peninsula by the complex group referred to as the "Moors" in 711 AD. Legend has it that the Visigoths, the rulers of Spain at the time, lost their empire in this last wave of initial Muslim expansion because of moral weakness. Nevertheless,

Spanish Christians in politics and the military throughout the Middle Ages viewed Moorish control as an intrusion on what was inherently theirs. They felt a deep obligation to "reconquer" political control of the land. In practice, this often meant living with their "enemies" and engaging in multilayered cultural exchange with them, from the court to the market and even to the joint construction of religious buildings.

Because medieval race and religion were constructed in ways completely different than they are in modern society (see Kaufman and Sturtevant for extensive resources and an introduction to the effects this has on modern discourse), it's relatively easy for the castellan's wife to see through her enemies' aggression to their shared humanity in my version of the miracle. Mentioning that Muslim tradition holds Mary, mother of Jesus, in high regard, here (l. 87) and in *Cantiga* 233 (l. 42), the medieval poets acknowledge common ground. For the poets, the Moorish and Christian military forces are mainly separated by historical circumstance, which can easily be overcome with a little goodwill.

A discussion of the thirteenth-century sociopolitical pressures on the historical castellan of Chincoya can be found in *Law and Order in Medieval Spain* (Knauss, *Law and Order* 162- 171). On a reader-response level, the character Sancho is hard to sympathize with because his actions are clearly misguided and dangerous. Indeed, after his humiliating capture in panel 8, the illustrations don't depict him again (Figure 6), and the poem similarly fails to mention him after he asks Chincoya to surrender, ignoring him for the final six stanzas.

I needed to create a main character who could hold onto readers' sympathy throughout the plot. Although the castellan in *Cantiga* 185 appears to be a bachelor, I was inspired by the

Figure 5: *Cantiga* 185, page 1. Escorial manuscript T.I.1.

188

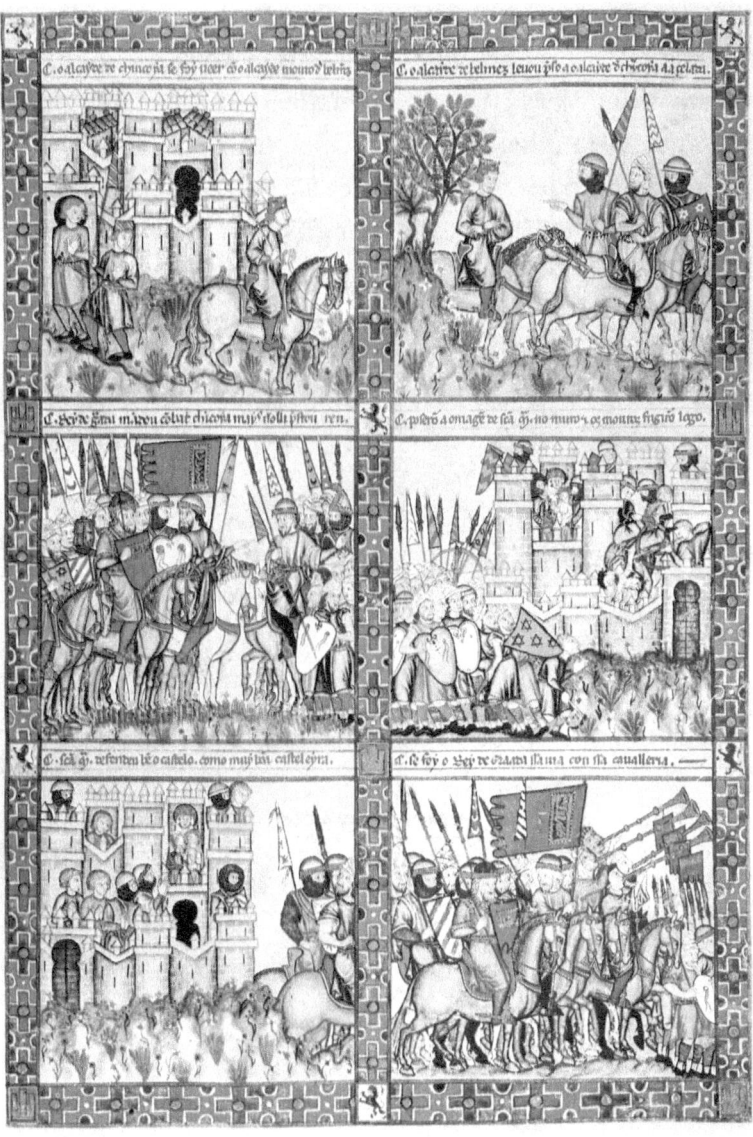

Figure 6: *Cantiga* 185, page 2. Escorial manuscript T.I.1.

189

Alfonsine injunction against a man who has been granted a royal village or fort ever abandoning the property, even if enemies kidnap or murder his wife and children (*Espéculo* 2.7.4.c). The wife and new mother in my adaptation has been abandoned by her husband to defend the king's castle and a minimal garrison with faith alone. It's a good thing she's in a *cantiga*, where everything always works out for the faithful.

Our Lady's Troubadour: *Cantiga* 194

Just as the name of the Virgin is beautiful to the good,
against the bad, it is very powerful and very fearful.

The poet of this *cantiga* doesn't mention whether he heard about the miracle or read it in a book, and no possible written sources have been identified. The *Códice rico* is missing several folios at the end, so although it likely originally included every song through *Cantiga* 200, 194 is the last *cantiga* illustrated in the manuscript (Figure 7). I especially admire panel 2, in which the jongleur entertains an apparently appreciative audience, and panel 4, in which the robbers literally take everything he has, even the tunic off his back. In panel 6, the jongleur triumphantly rides away, carrying his tunic without getting dressed again in his hurry to leave the attackers frozen.

The placement of the miracle in "Catalonna" (l. 5), as well as the wilderness depicted in the last four panels, suggested to me the rugged mountain areas of Catalunya, where robbers would have an unfair advantage over lone travelers.

Catalunya was part of the Kingdom of Aragón, which was ruled by Alfonso X's father-in-law, Jaume I, and then his brother-in-law, Pere III, in the thirteenth century. Munio makes reference to his home in Navarra. This was another separate kingdom in the north of the Iberian Peninsula with strong political and cultural ties to the Crown of Castile. In the thirteenth century, and especially in the context of Alfonso X's unification policy, these kingdoms maintained friendly relations, and many (Castilian) writers of the time were already thinking of these

Figure 7: *Cantiga* 194. Escorial manuscript T.I.1.

disparate lands as part of the single unit of "Spain." A traveling jongleur like Munio could've plied his trade with a reasonable expectation of safety. The mountains, however... Only the Mother of God could protect someone in those notorious spots.

Munio sings my translation of the refrain of *Cantiga* 29 when he's riding through the mountains. All of the other characters he mentions in this story come from medieval Spanish epic poems, and El Cid is considered to have been the "best seller." *The Song of the Cid* survives in only one manuscript, dated 1207, and is based on the life of a historical person, Ruy Díaz de Vivar (c. 1043–1099), who had an important role at court during the infancy of the Kingdom of Castile in the eleventh century. Indeed, medieval Spanish people seem to have preferred factual historical material for their entertainment, as all the songs mentioned in this story are traceable to possible historical events. This no-nonsense frame of mind is one reason why the *Cantigas* miracles are generally so down to earth, contextualized, and believable.

This is far from the only time St. Mary suddenly paralyzes attackers in the *Cantigas*. I chose this instance in order to write about a traveling musician, as music is so important to the *Cantigas*. The story lent its title to this commemorative anthology because in the wider context, "Our Lady's Troubadour" refers to Alfonso X himself.

Tournament of Honor: *Cantiga* 195

The Most Glorious One
must be merciful
to whomever keeps her feast and day
in any way they can

This miracle has three possible surviving sources, one English and two French in origin. It's another example of the cultural exchange between Spain and southern France. Its *cantiga's* text is longer than average, with twenty-five stanzas, and it should have two full pages of illustration in the *Códice rico*. While that manuscript conserves the musical notation and text, the artwork has been lost. There are plenty of examples of knights and nuns in other *cantigas*, sometimes in the same frame (Figure 8), so it would be simple to reconstruct a plausible approximation to the lost material in the manner demonstrated by Charles L. Nelson.

María sings part of the refrain of *Cantiga* 10, which is the first song of praise in the *Cantigas* collection and one of the most beautiful. It confirms the troubadour persona King Alfonso established in the Prologue and elevates St. Mary above all other possible loves with a metaphor that makes use of her emblem, the rose. Roses have evolved through horticulture to become full and multipetaled. In the thirteenth century, roses were more like today's rock roses, flat like daisies and usually with only five petals—five like St. Mary's number.

The medieval audience of the poem would've taken the knight's fate as a happy ending, because in spite of his sins, he is clearly favored by St. Mary and accepted into Paradise.

Figure 8: *Cantiga* 59, panel 1, showing a nun and a knight
at the convent door. *Cantiga* 195 has no surviving illustrations.
Escorial manuscript T.I.1.

Additionally, modern audiences likely agree that María's ending
is happy because she gets what she wants, and the abbess isn't
going to bother her anymore. The miracle is complex in the
medieval text, including both St. Mary's appearance in María's
dreams and the knight's redemption. I would add Don Ordoño's
sudden domination of his lascivious desires to the miraculous
occurrences in this tale.

195

Figure 9: *Cantiga* 207. Florence manuscript BR 20.

The Right Revenge: *Cantiga* 207

This isn't the first time I've written about New Saint Mary, a fascinating building in the historic quarter of Zamora, Spain. In the *Trout Riot* legend, the son in danger is named Pedro, which heavily influenced my choice of name for Don Fortún's son.

In contrast with *Cantiga* 195's length, *Cantiga* 207 is the shortest miracle poem in the collection. I present my translation of the entire original text to show the extent of the elements I've added to each story:

Refrain: *If a man willingly does a favor for the Virgin, she'll give him signs that it pleases her.*

I'll tell you a miracle about this, and you'll enjoy it.
St. Mary performed it with mercy and love
for a very good knight, her loyal servant,
who put his heart and mind into serving her.

He had a son he loved more than himself,
and a knight killed him. With grief
for his son, he seized (the knight) and
    wanted to kill him
where he'd killed his son, but he couldn't.

Taking him prisoner, he entered a church,
and the prisoner followed him,
    but he forgot about (the prisoner).

When he saw the image of the Virgin there,
he freed (the prisoner),
and the image bowed and said, "Thank you," for it.

The succinct poet didn't indicate where or when this miracle took place. I felt free to set it where I live, the beautiful medieval city of Zamora, because I wanted to provide vivid descriptions where the poet hadn't. I hope they bring Don Fortún's experience closer to the reader and make for an emotionally evocative tale.

A page of illustrations survives for this *cantiga* without captions in the F manuscript (Figure 9). The artists seem to have had some trouble interpreting who the recipient of the miracle was, perhaps due to the few details provided in the poem. The first panel establishes a man's devotion to St. Mary, a sure signal that he's the protagonist. But in panel 2, we see that this man is the murderer. In the following panels, the dead boy's father, my Fortún, is portrayed unsympathetically with his face covered by chainmail and in a position of threatening power over the established protagonist. I would agree with the artists that the miracle affects Blas the most, because it's his life that's spared, except that the poem is clearly told in sympathy with Fortún and his tremendous grief, and, most importantly, the supernatural thanks are directed toward him. The illustrations of *Cantiga* 207 are clear evidence of the independence of the jobs in the royal scriptorium, creating dialog and even contradictions between the different media in the finished product.

No-Man's-Land: *Cantiga* 233

*Those who die a good death and are free of sins
are with God and His Mother and always obey their
commands.*

This is another miracle that takes place close to home for the
Cantigas artists, and there are no known previous versions. The
original is oriented in a vague past, so I decided to set the story
in the eleventh century. Peñacoba, the site of the hermitage
referred to in the *cantiga*, is in the modern province of Burgos
and wouldn't have been near a border contested with Muslim
kingdoms at any later time in history.

The time period suggests that these knights are fighting for
King Fernando I, just after Castile was promoted from a county
of the Kingdom of León to its own separate kingdom. The
monastery of San Sebastián in this story is now known as the
famous Santo Domingo de Silos. The *cantiga* starts in medias
res, saying that the protagonist killed a lot of people, and one
day his enemies happened upon him on the road. I hope giving
Don Jacinto a reason to be in the dangerous canyon deepens the
psychology and helps the reader root for him.

Cantiga 233 has always held a special fascination for me,
perhaps because of the supernatural element. It was the first
cantiga I tried adapting for modern use. Before I started
studying for my PhD, I created a short and ponderous film
script based on this miracle, arguing that cinema was the only
appropriate "translation" for the multimedia *Cantigas de Santa
Maria*. Sometime after I'd finished my PhD as well as the first

draft of *Seven Noble Knights*, I returned to *Cantiga* 233. That story became a seed that germinated slowly and has only now blossomed into this book.

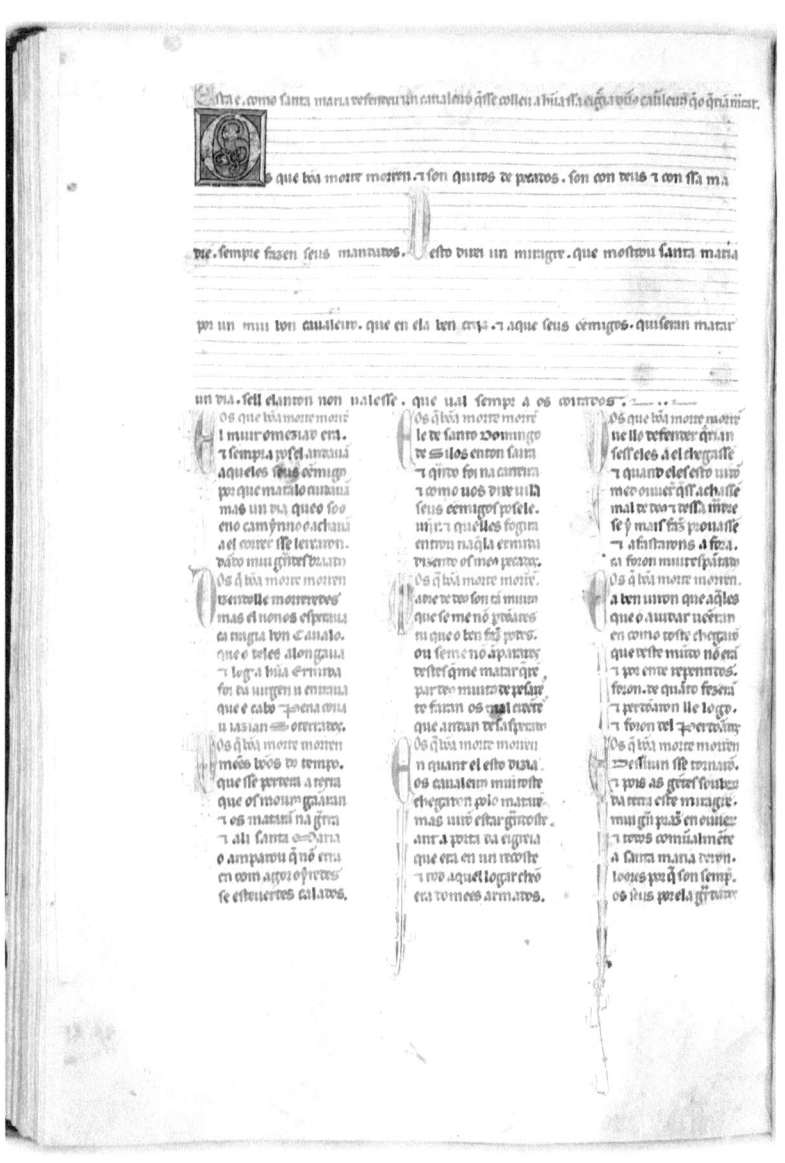

Figure 10: *Cantiga* 233 has full text, a decorated initial, and musical staves laid out, but the folio next to it, where its illustrations would have been, has been torn out. Florence manuscript BR 20.

Figure 11: The incomplete page intended to illustrate *Cantiga* 321. Florence manuscript BR 20.

Clear Water: *Cantiga* 321

In very little time, the Holy Queen heals
those whom medicine can cure very late or never.

It's no coincidence that this *cantiga* takes place in southern Spain, features King Alfonso X as a character, and is the first time the miracle was written down. Although, like most medieval Spanish monarchs, his was an itinerant court, Alfonso X spent half his thirty-two-year reign in Sevilla, now the capital of Andalusia. The king had a special interest in maintaining political control over the region he helped his father, Fernando III, *el Santo*, conquer for Castile, and living near the border with Granada and the ports of Andalusia offered strategic advantages.

I chose to adapt this miracle because the poets set it in Córdoba, where I first learned about Alfonso X and the *Cantigas*. I was only too happy to use my intimate knowledge of the historic quarter and the distance from the unique Mosque-Cathedral to the royal palace. Ballesteros-Beretta (*Itinerario*) places Alfonso X in Córdoba in 1265, which is an ideal year for the story because Prince Fernando was young and learning how to be king, and it was before the tragic events of the 1270s soured Alfonso's outlook. In 1265, the king would've been emotionally available to help a desperate widowed mother who, in the end, wasn't asking for a lot.

I also wanted to include the miraculous cure of a contagious illness in order to bring some of the healing power of the *Cantigas* worldview to the COVID-19 pandemic. Scrofula is a disease that can still be caught today. Tuberculosis bacteria settle outside the lungs, usually as in this story, in the lymph nodes, and cause painful swelling and blistering on the neck. With the treatment options available in the Middle Ages, it could easily have been fatal.

The disease was common enough at the time *Cantiga* 321 was written that England and France, and possibly other cultures, had developed scrofula-centered folklore based on the otherworldly powers of their monarchs (Montoya, "'Põer'"). The pragmatic Spanish spirit allows Alfonso X to laugh off the magical suggestion and direct his subjects to a treatment which, in his ideal kingdom, cannot fail, thus fulfilling his role as intermediary between St. Mary and his people.

Faded Threads: *Cantiga* 341

Just as the Virgin is aggrieved by those who sin,
she also fights to save those who haven't
committed any crime.

Location is paramount in this *cantiga*. The geography of Mont St. Michel at Le-Puy-en-Velay practically writes its own stories about dramatic jumps and terrible falls. Tales of innocent people surviving trials by ordeal fascinated listeners throughout the Middle Ages, so it's puzzling that, according to Stephen Parkinson, after the *Cantigas* version, "The earliest extant version of this miracle, referring to the chapel dedicated to St. Michael on the Aiguilhe rock in Puy-le-Velay, dates from the sixteenth century" ("Alfonso X" 98).

This is the second story I wrote, years ago, with the idea of someday adding more and making a book. It came about shortly after I finished "No-Man's-Land." I'd been writing historical fiction from a masculine point of view, so I sought a refreshing feminine perspective. During my days as a student, certain lines of *Cantiga* 341 deeply impressed me:

> *And many times, she was mistreated and badly*
> *injured by him,*
> *and she had little to eat, and also went about poorly*
> *dressed,*
> *since that's the kind of life women with jealous*
> *husbands live.* (l. 16–18, my translation)

Nowadays, we know it's wrong to accept that anyone should be treated this way. In contrast, the medieval song has to explain that the woman is a devotee of St. Mary and has never given her husband reason to doubt her faithfulness to him, and that's why her husband is in the wrong. The *cantiga's* protagonist confronts her husband, explicitly reasoning that people who've committed no crime shouldn't be punished, but only after she's already suffered far too much.

I shuddered to imagine what it would be like to live in a society in which women had no recourse against conjugal abuse, and I wanted to reclaim the story by telling it from the wife's point of view and giving her a support network that helps her find the courage to stand up for herself. The line about being poorly dressed inspired Raoul's occupation, since it would be much harder to hide having no new clothes if Caterine is married to the town tailor.

The husband in the *cantiga* sees the error of his ways, just as Raoul does. Although it's not a practical solution in today's real world, his wife forgives him, and they live happily ever after, since all *cantigas* have happy endings.

Unlike any of the other stories, I wrote this *cantiga* in the present tense. It seems appropriate to end this commemorative collection with a symbolic acknowledgment of the way these stories are still relevant, eight hundred years later.

Sources and Further Reading

Alfonso X, *el Sabio*. *Cantigas de Santa María*. 3 vols., edited by Walter Mettmann, Clásicos Castalia, 1986–1989.

——. *Cantigas de Santa María: Edición facsímil del códice T.I.1 de la Biblioteca de San Lorenzo el Real de El Escorial, siglo XIII*. Edilán, 1979.

——. *Cantigas de Santa María: Edición facsímil del códice B.R.20 de la Biblioteca Nazionale Centrale de Florencia, siglo XIII*. Edilán, 1989.

——. *Espéculo: Texto jurídico atribuido al Rey de Castilla don Alfonso X, el Sabio*. Edited and introduction by Robert A. MacDonald, Hispanic Seminary of Medieval Studies, 1990.

——. *Songs of Holy Mary of Alfonso X, the Wise: A Translation of the "Cantigas de Santa Maria."* Translated by Kathleen Kulp-Hill, Arizona Center for Medieval and Renaissance Studies, 2000.

Ballesteros-Beretta, Antonio. *Alfonso X, el Sabio*. El Albir, 1984.

—. *Itinerario de Alfonso X, rey de Castilla*, vol. 8, 1265–1267. Biblioteca Virtual Miguel de Cervantes, 2011. Digital edition based on *Boletín de la Real Academia de la Historia*, vol. 109, julio-septiembre 1936, pp. 377-460.

Burns, Robert I., ed. *Emperor of Culture: Alfonso X the Learned of Castile and His Thirteenth-Century Renaissance.* University of Pennsylvania Press, 1990.

The Cantigas de Santa Maria Database. Centre for the Study of the *Cantigas de Santa Maria* of Oxford University, 2005–, http://csm.mml.ox.ac.uk/.

Carpenter, Dwayne E. "Social Perception and Literary Portrayal: Jews and Muslims in Medieval Spanish Literature." *Convivencia: Jews, Muslims and Christians in Medieval Spain.* Edited by Vivian B. Mann, Thomas F. Glick, and Jerrilynn D. Dodds, George Braziller, The Jewish Museum, 1992, pp. 61-111.

Casson, Andrew. *"Cantigas de Santa Maria" for Singers*, 2019–, http://cantigasdesantamaria.com/.

Craddock, Jerry R. "Dynasty in Dispute: Alfonso el Sabio and the Succession to the Throne of Castile and Leon in History and Legend." *Viator*, vol. 16, 1986, pp. 197-219.

Dexter, Elise Forsythe. "Sources of the Cantigas of Alfonso el Sabio." PhD. Diss., U. Wisconsin, 1926.

Domínguez Rodríguez, Ana. "Algunas precisiones sobre el arte alfonsí." *El códice de Florencia de las Cantigas de Alfonso X el Sabio.* Volumen complementario de la edición facsímil del ms. B. R. 20 de la Biblioteca Nazionale de Florencia. Edilán, 1991, pp. 145-162.

Doubleday, Simon. *The Wise King: A Christian Prince, Muslim Spain, and the Birth of the Renaissance.* Basic Books, 2015.

Fidalgo, Elvira. *As Cantigas de Santa María.* Edicións Xerais de Galicia, 2002.

Fita, Fidel. "Biografías de San Fernando y de Alfonso el Sabio por Gil de Zamora." *Boletín de la Real Academia de la Historia,* vol. 5, 1884, pp. 308-328.

Flory, David A. *Marian Representations in the Miracle Tales of Thirteenth-Century Spain and France.* Catholic University of America Press, 2000.

Greenia, George D. "The Court of Alfonso X in Words and Pictures: The *Cantigas.*" *Courtly Literature, Culture and Context: Selected Papers from the Fifth Triennial Congress of the International Courtly Literature Society, Dalfsen, The Netherlands, 9–16 August, 1986.* Edited by Keith Busby and Erik Kooper, John Benjamins, 1990, pp. 227-237.

Guerrero Lovillo, José, *Las Cántigas: Estudio arqueológico de sus miniaturas.* Consejo Superior de Investigaciones Científicas, 1949.

Katz, Israel J., and John Esten Keller, eds. *Studies on the 'Cantigas de Santa Maria': Art, Music, and Poetry: Proceedings of the International Symposium on the 'Cantigas de Santa Maria' of Alfonso X, el Sabio (1221–1284) in Commemoration of its 700ᵗʰ Anniversary Year—1981.* Hispanic Seminary of Medieval Studies, 1987.

Kaufman, Amy S., and Paul B. Sturtevant. *The Devil's Historians: How Modern Extremists Abuse the Medieval Past.* University of Toronto Press, 2020.

Keller, John Esten. "Drama, Ritual and Incipient Opera in Alfonso's *Cantigas.*" In Burns, *Emperor of Culture,* pp. 72-89.

—. "The Living Corpse: Miracle 67 of the *Cantigas de Santa Maria* of Alfonso X." *Bulletin of the Cantigueiros de Santa Maria,* vol. 2, 1988–1989, pp. 55-68.

—. "The Motif of the Statue Bride in the *Cantigas* of Alfonso the Learned." *Studies in Philology,* vol. 56, 1959, pp. 453-458.

Keller, John Esten, and Annette Grant Cash. *Daily Life Depicted in the "Cantigas de Santa Maria."* University Press of Kentucky, 1998.

Keller, John Esten, and Richard P. Kincade. *Iconography in Medieval Spanish Literature.* University Press of Kentucky, 1984.

Knauss, Jessica. *Law and Order in Medieval Spain: Alfonsine Legislation and the* Cantigas de Santa Maria. Açedrex Publishing, 2011.

Knauss, J. K. *Trout Riot: A Legend from Zamora, Spain, in Eight Scenes.* Açedrex Publishing, 2020.

Menéndez Pidal, Gonzalo. "Cómo trabajaron las escuelas alfonsíes." *Nueva Revista de Filología Hispánica,* vol. 5, no. 4, 1951, pp. 363-380.

—. "Los manuscritos de las Cantigas: Cómo se elaboró la

miniatura alfonsí." *Boletín de la Real Academia de la Historia*, vol. 150, 1962, pp. 26-58.

Montoya Martínez, Jesús. *Historia y anécdotas de Andalucía en las Cantigas de Santa María de Alfonso X*. Universidad de Granada, 1988.

—. "'Põer as mãos sobre os lamparões'; reminiscencias del milagro regio: toucher les écrouelles (CSM 321)." *Exemplaria Hispanica*, vol. 2, 1992–1993, pp. 125-134.

—. "El Puerto de Santa María, exvoto de Alfonso X a María." *Alcanate: Revista de Estudios Alfonsíes*, vol. I, 1998–1999, pp. 99-114.

Nelson, Charles L. "Art and Visualization in the *Cantigas de Santa Maria*: How the Artists Worked." In Katz and Keller, *Studies on the CSM*, pp. 111-134.

O'Callaghan, Joseph F. *Alfonso X and the Cantigas de Santa Maria: A Poetic Biography*. Brill, 1998.

—. "The Ideology of Government in the Reign of Alfonso X of Castile." *Exemplaria Hispanica*, vol. 1, 1991–1992, pp. 1-17.

—. *The Learned King: The Reign of Alfonso X of Castile*. University of Pennsylvania Press, 1993.

Parkinson, Stephen. "Alfonso X, Miracle Collector." *Alfonso X El Sabio 1221-1284, Las Cantigas de Santa María, Códice Rico, Ms. T-I-1, Real Biblioteca del Monasterio de San Lorenzo de El Escorial*, vol. II, edited by Laura Fernández Fernández and Juan Carlos Ruiz Sousa, Testimonio, 2011, pp. 79-105.

—. "*Meestria métrica*: Metrical virtuosity in the *Cantigas de Santa Maria*." *La corónica*, vol. 27, no. 2, Spring 1999, pp. 21-35.

—. "Miragres de maldizer?: Dysphemism in the *Cantigas de Santa Maria*." *Bulletin of the Cantigueiros de Santa Maria*, vol. 4, 1992, pp. 44-57.

Presilla, Maricel E. "The Image of Death in the 'Cantigas de Santa Maria' of Alfonso X (1252–1284): The Politics of Death and Salvation." PhD. Diss. New York University, 1989.

Salvador Martínez, H. *Alfonso X, el Sabio: Una biografía*. Ediciones Polifemo: 2003.

Scarborough, Connie L. "Alfonso X: Monarch in Search of a Miracle." *Romance Quarterly*, vol. 33, no. 3, 1986, pp. 349-354.

—. *A Holy Alliance: Alfonso X's Political Use of Marian Poetry*. Juan de la Cuesta, 2009.

Snow, Joseph T. "Alfonso as Troubadour: The Fact and the Fiction." In Burns, *Emperor of Culture*, pp. 124-140.

—. "Alfonso X y las *Cantigas*: documento personal y poesía colectiva." *El Scriptorium alfonsí: de los Libros de Astrología a las "Cantigas de Santa María."* Edited by Jesús Montoya Martínez and Ana Domínguez Rodríguez, Editorial Complutense, 1999, pp. 159-172.

—. "The Central Rôle of the Troubadour *Persona* of Alfonso X in the *Cantigas de Santa Maria*." *Bulletin of Hispanic Studies*, vol. 66, 1979, pp. 305-316.

—. "Poetic Self-Awareness in Alfonso X's *Cantiga* 110." *Kentucky Romance Quarterly*, vol. 26, 1979, pp. 421-432.

—. "Self-Conscious References and the Organic Narrative Pattern of the CSM." *Medieval, Renaissance and Folklore Studies in Honor of John Esten Keller.* Edited by Joseph R. Jones, Juan de la Cuesta, 1980, pp. 53-66.

Solalinde, Antonio G. "Intervención de Alfonso X en la redacción de sus obras." *Revista de Filología Española*, vol. 2, 1915, pp. 283-288.

Acknowledgments

I'm indebted to the following people for encouraging my single-minded pursuit of all things Alfonsine.

Joseph T. Snow arrived for a visit to the Brown campus during my first year of PhD study and, probably unwittingly, gave me a sense of why it was worthwhile to push through imposter syndrome and other demons to write my dissertation on the *Cantigas*.

Mercedes Vaquero's remark, "Te gusta contar historias, ¿no?" provided sufficient direction for my life after graduate school.

My dear departed husband, Stanley Arthur Coombs, listened to *Cantigas* recordings with me and supported me in every way during the writing of "No-Man's-Land" and "Faded Threads."

Debra J. H. Bolton honored my Alfonsine academic work, giving me an unsolicited and necessary push in this creative avenue of honoring Alfonso's legacy.

Connie Scarborough was unfailingly helpful with everything I pestered her about in spite of our mutual disappointment about the postponement and loss of most Alfonsine commemorations in 2021.

Daniel Sanz Martín gamely took me to visit the sites of *Cantigas*-related sanctuaries in every weather condition imaginable and went far out of his way to obtain the figures in this book taken from the facsimile held at the Archivo Municipal de Burgos.

Fernando Pérez Fernández fueled my writerly passion with an uncomfortable couch, *cocido, fabada, pollo a la cerveza*, strategic supportive compliments, and matter-of-fact resourcefulness in times of crisis.

The Low Writers of Tucson, Arizona, stuck together through job changes and a pandemic and consistently pointed out medieval details that seem normal to me but probably not to my potential readers.

The crack team at Encircle Publications had faith in my writing.

This collection wouldn't exist without you.

Thank you. Gracias. Graças.

About the Author

J. K. Knauss graduated as valedictorian of her class with multiple honors from Wheaton College in Norton, Massachusetts. She first seriously studied the works of Alfonso X, *el Sabio*, for her MA in medieval studies at the University of Leeds, England. She earned her PhD in medieval Spanish literature from Brown University with a dissertation that has been published as *Law and Order in Medieval Spain: Alfonsine Legislation and the* Cantigas de Santa Maria. In the course of her academic career, she has studied and researched in Córdoba, Sevilla, and Salamanca, Spain.

She's worked as a librarian and a teacher of Spanish and English as well as an editor at small presses. She helped found Loose Leaves Publishing as well as Açedrex Publishing, and now does bilingual editing in Spain.

She's the author of another tribute to Alfonso X's literary legacy, the critically acclaimed medieval epic *Seven Noble Knights* (Encircle Publications, 2020). Her 2012 translation of *The Abencerraje* has been adopted as a college textbook, she contributed a story to the bestselling anthology *We All Fall Down: Stories of Plague and Resilience* (2020), and published a one-act play based on a Zamoran legend, *Trout Riot* (2020).

Writing as Jessica Knauss, she's also the author of the "quirky, intriguing" novella *Tree/House* (2008), "exuberant, never cloying" *Dusk Before Dawn: Poems* (2010), the contemporary paranormal *Awash in Talent* (Kindle Press, 2016), and the science fantasy novella *The Atwells Avenue Anomaly* (2021). Many of her contemporary short stories and flash fiction have been published in literary magazines. She collected these short works in *Unpredictable Worlds: Stories* (2015), which has been compared to the works of Bradbury, Kipling, Saki, and O. Henry. Her translation of Lidia Falcón's *Camino sin retorno* was published as *No Turning Back* (Loose Leaves Publishing, 2013).

Visit her website, www.JessicaKnauss.com.

If you enjoyed reading this book,
please consider writing your honest review
and sharing it with other readers.

Many of our Authors are happy to participate in
Book Club and Reader Group discussions.
For more information, contact us at info@encirclepub.com.

Thank you,
Encircle Publications

For news about more exciting new fiction, join us at:
Facebook: www.facebook.com/encirclepub

Twitter: twitter.com/encirclepub

Instagram: www.instagram.com/encirclepublications

Sign up for Encircle Publications newsletter and specials:
eepurl.com/cs8taP

www.ingramcontent.com/pod-product-compliance
Lightning Source LLC
Chambersburg PA
CBHW050316110726
47899CB00007B/2270